PRAISE

"Thor, Baldacci, Flynn, Hamburg. Get ready as Banner fits right in!"

AMAZON REVIEW

"Move over Jack Reacher there's a new guy taking over."

AMAZON REVIEW

"Great stuff. Exciting and fast paced. On par with Flynn & Thor."

AMAZON REVIEW

"The writing was superior, the story line was compelling and the action was top-notch. Sorry I could only give this one a five star rating!"

AMAZON REVIEW

BLOOD ON BALTHAZAR

A HARRY BAUER THRILLER

BLAKE BANNER

RIGHTHOUSE

The characters and events portrayed in this ebook are fictitious. Any similarity to real persons, living or dead, is coincidental and not intended by the author.

ISBN-13: 978-1-63696-323-5

ISBN-10: 1-63696-323-4

Cover design by: Damonza

Printed in the United States of America

www.righthouse.com

www.instagram.com/righthousebooks

www.facebook.com/righthousebooks

twitter.com/righthousebooks

HARRY BAUER THRILLER SERIES

Dead of Night (Book 1)
Dying Breath (Book 2)
The Einstaat Brief (Book 3)
Quantum Kill (Book 4)
Immortal Hate (Book 5)
The Silent Blade (Book 6)
LA: Wild Justice (Book 7)
Breath of Hell (Book 8)
Invisible Evil (Book 9)
The Shadow of Ukupacha (Book 10)
Sweet Razor Cut (Book 11)
Blood of the Innocent (Book 12)
Blood on Balthazar (Book 13)
Simple Kill (Book 14)
Riding The Devil (Book 15)
The Unavenged (Book 16)
The Devil's Vengeance (Book 17)
Bloody Retribution (Book 18)
Rogue Kill (Book 19)
Blood for Blood (Book 20)

ONE

The sky was a sheet of clean, blue ice. I was on US Route 1, in Maine. My GPS had told me to follow the I-95 to Bangor, but I wanted to lose myself. That was what the trip was about: losing myself and seeing if I could find another me I liked better.

So at Brunswick I had taken Route 1 and ambled through Rockland, Belfast, Searsport and Ellsworth, smelling the rich ozone of the North Atlantic, allowing the dappled green shade of the newborn leaves to soothe my soul. Spring was yawning and stretching in the pinewoods and in the meadows.

I had the soft top down on my brand-new, twenty-year-old TVR Chimera. While it was cruising it made a noise like a Harley on steroids, but when you put your foot down, the 340 hp Rover V8 would give you naught to sixty in less than four seconds while screaming like a host of blood-crazed daemons out of Hell. However, that day in late March I was all about leaving the daemons behind and finding something like peace. The sea, gliding past on my right, was dark and still, overlooked by a scattering of cute, clapboard houses set among an abundance of new flowers and budding trees; and the Chimera was uttering nothing more than a reassuring rumble.

The air was cold, but even that was good. It was like a wake-up call, a cold shower on a fresh morning. Life, not death, was the message.

I had left Manhattan at three that morning. My GPS told me I'd arrive at the small town of Balthazar, six miles north of Machias, Maine, at noon. I had taken my time and enjoyed the drive, but as it was, with the empty roads, it was closer to eleven thirty when I turned north onto the Stony Lake Road and left Machias behind me. Six miles and five minutes after that I crossed the Jebediah O'Hanlon Memorial Bridge over the Stony River and entered Balthazar along Main Street. A sharp left after the bridge brought me onto green and leafy Water Street. A large, three-story building on the corner, in duck-egg blue, advertised a pottery and a fine arts and antique shop. The ochre yellow, clapboard building next door offered tea, coffee and cakes, and also help with your computer. Quaint.

I cruised down Water Street, among the dappled shade and March sunlight, noticing that the people I saw were mostly not walking, but had paused to talk to somebody—a neighbor, an acquaintance or a friend. I thought maybe that was important.

Only very recently I had stood and shot a woman in the head. She had been a very bad, very cruel woman. The ethos of the organization I worked for was that the world was a better place because she was no longer in it. But for just a second, as I drove past the Water Street Tea and Coffee House, where two women stood talking in the spring morning sunshine, I wondered what they had been doing at the moment I shot Rafaela. Perhaps they had been sharing apples, milk or butter, or helping each other to clear the snow from their driveways. And I wondered if what I had done in that moment had been more valuable than what they had done. Which of us had actually made the world a slightly better place?

The thought was impossible to answer, and a few moments later I pulled up outside the cottage I had rented for the month of March. It was a gunmetal gray, clapboard, two-story cottage with a gabled, slate roof and a chimney pot. It had an unkempt lawn front and back and to the sides, and it was surrounded by oaks and a couple of huge sycamores.

There was a red Toyota pulled up out front, so I pulled in beside it, killed the engine and climbed out. As I slammed the door, the door to the house opened.

She was in a red skirt with a bright red jacket and a white, frilly blouse. She was in her mid thirties and pretty in a demure way, with her hair pulled into a bun at the back of her neck and long earrings that made her neck look nice. She was already smiling, so I smiled back.

"Mr. Bauer!" She said it smiling like I really *shouldn't* have. "I *do* hope you had a good trip. Please, come on in and let me show you around. Can I help you with your bags?"

I told her that wasn't necessary and followed her inside while she continued talking.

"You didn't, um..." She paused and flashed me a smile. "You weren't very..." In the end she decided the thing was to blame herself. "I didn't quite catch exactly how long... I mean, you paid for the month in advance, and that's wonderful, but I wasn't clear..."

We were in a big, spacious room with wooden floors and heavy rugs. There was an open fireplace with a big, stone chimney breast, the walls were paneled in wood up to hip height, there were cottagey armchairs and a sofa set around a bay window, and at the far end of the room an oval dining table with six chairs, a second fireplace and a set of triple-glazed doors out onto a lawn.

I nodded and gave her another noncommittal smile. "I needed to get away from work—and from New York for a while. I don't know how long." I extended the smile to a grin. "I won't be here next year, but if you need to kick me out, that won't be a problem."

She was scandalized, fluttered and laughed while I went to look at the kitchen, and the bedrooms upstairs.

"Anything at all you need," she told me several times in several different parts of the house as I looked around, "just call me. You have my number."

Back down in the living room I told her, "Somewhere I can have some lunch, I haven't eaten since five AM."

She laughed like I was the wittiest thing since Oscar Wilde. "Well, we have no restaurants like the ones you must be used to in Manhattan! But Helen's is a friendly, family-oriented place with home-cooked food and *very* generous portions!"

She hurried to the door, stepped out onto the porch and pointed along the road. The wind tried to flap her skirt, but it was too tight, so it dragged her hair across her face instead.

"There, just at the end of the road," she said. "You can't miss it!"

I waved to her as she pulled away in her bright red Toyota, then carried my bags up to the master bedroom. I hung my clothes in the freestanding oak wardrobe, which was big enough for three witches, a cauldron and a stake, showered and changed and took the Chimera for a short drive in the spring sunshine, up to Helen's Family Restaurant.

Like most of the buildings in Balthazar, it was white clapboard with a gabled slate roof, but instead of being set among lawns and trees, like the rest of the town, it was set on the water's edge on Stony Lake, in the midst of a parking lot that would probably have been suitable for the Super Bowl. The nearest buildings were the Lakeside Motel and an ATM which were about fifty and a hundred and fifty yards away respectively. You got the feeling space was not a problem up here. Lots of space and few people. And that was OK with me.

I pushed through the big glass doors. It was warm inside. There was a counter with stools along the far wall, and there were maybe a dozen round, wooden tables scattered around the room. Half of them were occupied and there was a warm buzz of quiet conversation and laughter.

Up at the bar there was a couple, maybe in their mid-forties, with a bunch of kids around them. The kids were mid to late teens. When you live in a city like New York you learn to see teenagers as a possible risk, to be treated with caution, and you sure as hell don't talk to them because most of them have forgotten how to talk. But these kids were talking recognizable English, some were laughing, and a couple of them had their arms around the two adults. A physical resemblance suggested they were family. I tried not to stare and sat at a table by the window, thinking maybe this was what humans were like when you took them out of the hive.

A cute woman with blonde hair and humorous, naughty eyes came over with a notepad.

"Hello!" She said it like we'd grown up together and she hadn't seen me since we were kids. The accent wasn't New England. "I'm Helen. Passing through? What can I get you?"

"If you bring me a great steak and fries and a good cold beer, I might stay..."

"Oh, well I'll see what I can do, Mr...."

"Name's Harry."

"All right, Harry! I'll be right back."

She went away and the conversation that was going on at the bar spread to a couple of the tables. The one who was doing most of the talking was a pretty girl of about sixteen. She was a blonde with very blue eyes and a big personality. She was laughing and speaking to a couple sitting at a table by the door.

"We *are* going. This will *not* be the first time in over one hundred years that we don't do the March Mom March! It's less than three miles, just a couple of hours' walk. It's not like we're climbing Everest!"

The man at the table was a big, genial-looking guy with heavy glasses and shaggy hair. He was managing to smile and look worried at the same time.

"All I'm saying, Suzy, is be careful. The snow is comin' in and it looks like it could be heavy. Three miles can be a hell of a long way in two or three feet of snow at fifteen or twenty degrees. I'm tellin' you, heavy snow can be real dangerous." He shifted his attention to the woman who was hugging the girl. "Not for me to interfere, Emma..."

The man beside her replied. "No, you're right, Bob. We'll keep an eye on the weather report. Snow's usually gone by this time in March..."

"Well, that's what worries me, Ned. Shouldn't be snow at this time. Bit of sleet at most. But this is comin' down out a' New Brunswick with a vengeance."

"I seen it on the news. We'll keep an eye on it."

I glanced at the other kids. There were a couple of other girls of about the same age. They looked like cheerleaders, fit, athletic, pretty. The boys were male versions of the girls, all-American football players, eager for a challenge. They were full of bravado. Three miles of snow was not going to stop them.

Helen came over with a cold beer, a steak that was bigger than the plate and a basket full of fries.

I sat back and smiled. "You'll have to direct me to the nearest realtor. I think I died and went to Maine." She laughed and I asked her, "So what is the March Mom March?"

"Oh, most years, since..." She looked over at the group at the counter. Suzy interrupted her.

"*Every* year since 1908! That's one hundred and twelve years!"

"OK, *every* year since 1908, the teenagers of Balthazar have done a trek to Stony Lake, because there is a meadow there, by the water, which grows a mass of sweet white violets. They pick basket loads of them and they bring them back and decorate City Hall Square and the statue of Emily Jones with them, and they call it the March Mom March."

"Why's that?"

"Well, traditionally, they celebrated the last Sunday in March as Emily Jones Day. She was the wife of Balthazar Jones, who founded the town, and she did wonderful work with children. That was before independence, and so she was commemorated on English Mothering Sunday. So the flowers were to honor Emily Jones, and also the town mothers."

"That's nice."

"Yeah, but this year we have a big snowstorm coming down from Canada and some people are saying the march should be cancelled."

The family at the bar and the couple at the table had all turned to watch Helen while she spoke. When she'd finished they all looked at me, like I should contribute my opinion. I glanced at the kids and smiled.

"When do you go?"

Suzy snapped back, "This afternoon. We camp there and come back tomorrow."

I gave my head a twitch. "You all look pretty strong and healthy to me. But I'd have to agree with Bob over there." I gave him a nod. "I've had to work in snow sometimes. And I can tell you, in a snowstorm, out in the wilds, a mile—especially in difficult terrain—is a lot more than you need to get hypothermia. My advice, if you're bent on going, is make sure you have a good extraction plan in place."

Ned turned on his stool to look at me. "Extraction? You military?"

"Long time ago."

He nodded, then gestured at my steak. "Don't let us stop you eating, Harry. We'll take care of our kids." He'd dismissed me and now he turned to Bob. "Don't worry about it, Bob. We're not going to put our kids at risk."

I ate my steak and drank my beer, paid up and wished them a good day. They responded with a friendly chorus, but I didn't hear Ned's voice among them.

Outside I looked up at the sky. It was still a clear, perfect ice blue. But I knew well enough that on the Atlantic coast, especially this far north, the weather could change fast, within minutes. And where snow was concerned, what might normally be a short drive, could become a struggle for survival.

On the way home I stopped by the supermarket and stocked up on meat, fresh vegetables, bread, beer and whiskey, and any other essentials I could think of. When I pushed my trolley out of the store and into the parking lot the sky was still looking clear and blue, but over in the north, over the treetops and the rooftops, there was a line of heavy, irregular peaks you might have been forgiven for thinking were mountains. But they were not mountains, they were clouds.

A sudden, chill wind made me shudder as I opened the trunk, and as I started loading the groceries into the car, I found myself hoping the kids stayed at home that afternoon.

The drive home took me past the sheriff's office, the village hall and the county jail. They were all housed in a big, oddly sinister redbrick building with sharp, pointed roofs surrounded by tall poplar trees. On an impulse I stopped, climbed out of the TVR and pushed through the big glass doors. There was an elbow-high wooden counter and beyond it a couple of unoccupied desks. At the counter there was a man in a brown and beige uniform and a sheriff's star. He watched me with cautious eyes as I approached.

"My name is Harry Bauer, I'm renting the Willows, on Water Street, for the next month or so."

"Sheriff Walt Davies. Welcome to Balthazar, Mr. Bauer."

He made it sound like a caution, but I ignored his tone and went on.

"I was wondering about the snowstorm that's coming down out of Canada. Do we know what the status is on that?"

"Yup." He put some papers in a manila folder, dropped them on the desk behind him and then leaned on the counter with two powerful hands. "Unseasonable, heavy snow coming down from New Brunswick. Should reach us sometime tonight. It's going to reach fourteen degrees in the small hours, with northerly winds gusting to fifty miles per hour."

I thanked him and was about to leave but stopped. "I was at Helen's Restaurant earlier and got into a conversation with some people. Their kids were going on the March Mom March?" He nodded. "It's none of my business and I don't mean to interfere, but those kids seemed pretty young. Are they going to be all right?"

He lowered himself from his hands to his elbows and gave his head a sideways twitch. "Folks here know the weather and what the snow can do, Mr. Bauer. We live with it every winter. We've advised them to stay at home this year, but it's a free country. We can't stop them from going."

"Sure." I nodded. "Well, if it comes to it I have a lot of experience in search and rescue. I'd be happy to help out."

"'Preciate it. Let's hope it don't come to it."

I left the building and looked up at the sky. It was still full of the joys of spring, but away in the north the clouds were building into leaden mountains, and acquiring an inky darkness.

TWO

It came in the night, wild and loud, rattling at the doors and howling down the chimney. Through the black panes of glass in the windows all you could see was swirling, crazy ghosts in a freezing, lightless world. I got out of bed and made my way around the house, closing the wooden shutters over the windows and thinking about the kids trapped up by the lake. I hoped their parents had had the sense to go get them before the storm broke, or to stop them from going in the first place. Right then, there was nothing anyone could do. We could put a man on Mars, but we could not go three miles in the snow to rescue a bunch of crazy kids.

I slept till six, had a cold shower, dressed warm and took a walk to the sheriff's office. The wind had died down, but the snow was still coming down heavy. When I got there, there was warm yellow light spilling from the doors onto the thick white drifts outside. I pushed in, stamped my feet and found the sheriff leaning with his elbows on the counter, like he hadn't moved all night. He was listening to the woman called Emma, Suzy's mother. She was saying, "We have to go and get them, Walt."

He had his eyes closed and he was nodding, like she was being irrational and he was being patient.

"Now, Emma, I told you there is nothing we can do till the snow eases. Right now, we go out there, we ain't going to be no help to them, and we are going to need rescuing ourselves. We have to wait..." He turned to look at me like I was a recurring toothache. "Mr. Bauer, what can I do for you?"

"We need to go and get those kids. An hour in these conditions can be the difference between living and dying of hypothermia."

"We know that, Mr. Bauer. I don't know if you know this, but it snows quite a bit in northern Maine."

I leaned on the counter. "Have you ever spent the night hanging from a mountainside in a sleeping bag at minus forty degrees, Sheriff?" He sighed heavily. I pressed him, "Have you ever spent a month surviving in mountains at minus twenty, with nothing but a Bergen and a pound of chocolate?"

"No, Mr. Bauer, but no doubt you're going to tell us you have."

"In Afghanistan."

"Of course."

"It's not the same as watching the snow through a triple-glazed window, or fighting your way to the mall. And I am telling you that if we don't organize a party now, some of those kids are going to die."

"Now you listen to me, Mister Bauer, a thing like this needs to be organized. I need to call in search and rescue. We don't have the resources and I cannot just snap my fingers..."

I was getting bored so I cut across him. "Can you manage to organize some flasks of hot coffee and some blankets? I'll take them." I turned to Emma. "How many kids are there?"

"I think in the end only nine of them went. I can't bear to think of them out there on their own. Do you think you can help them?"

"Now hang on!"

I turned to him. "What for?"

"I cannot be responsible..."

"You are not going to be responsible, Sheriff. I am. Now, while we stand here arguing, there are kids out there who have spent over twelve hours in sub-freezing temperatures. We need to act. I need you to respond, Sheriff. Start making hot coffee and putting it in flasks. You want to lace it with some whiskey, that will help. You, Emma, start calling your friends and collecting blankets, maybe flasks of hot soup. And I'll need a big rucksack. We need to be doing this, not talking about it. Go."

She nodded a few times, then rushed out saying, "Yes, rucksack, soup, blankets..."

The door closed behind her and I turned to the sheriff, who was staring at me. I asked him, "Is this going to be a problem?"

He took a moment, then said, "It ain't, but something tells me you are."

"Thanks. Something tells me one of those nine kids isn't yours." He scowled. I ignored him. "You got any deputies?"

"You're getting on my nerves, Mr. Bauer. Yeah, I got a couple of deputies."

"Then how about you get them on the phone and organize them getting blankets, soup and coffee. I'm sorry, Sheriff. I just don't have the time to be polite."

He grunted and picked up the phone. As he dialed I asked him, "How far am I going to get in a truck?"

"Nowhere. Quarter of a mile past the Old Town Bridge. It's what I'm telling you. What you are proposing is suicide." He had the receiver to his ear. "Best thing we can do is stay put. The kids stay put and let Search and... Hank?" He said that into the phone. "Listen, I got a..." He glanced at me. "I got a volunteer here, says he has a lot of experience with search and rescue in snow and ice. He's going to take some blankets and hot drinks out to the kids..." He sighed as he listened, watching me. "Yeah, I know Hank, but he says he's done it before. So, just listen, will ya? Get brewing coffee. Go over to Helen's and get her to make some hot soup, and whatever blankets people can spare... Nine of them." He stared at me a little longer, then said, "Yeah, OK," and hung up. "Hank says he'll go with you."

I shook my head. "No, he'll slow me down. I don't need to be helping people—"

"Cut it out, will you, mister? He's strong and he's fit. You want to make everybody feel like shit around here? He's going with you and like as not you'll have a few dads signing up for your crazy-ass expedition."

"Good," I said, then smiled. "They can look after each other while I get to the kids."

"Yeah, right. I'm going to make coffee."

He gave me a sour look and made for the kitchenette at the back.

Over the next fifteen to twenty minutes people started showing up, pushing in out of the dark, stamping snow onto the floor. There were men, women, couples and even kids. Some brought rucksacks, others brought flasks of coffee and soup, blankets and even thermal underwear. A few deposited the things and left, most stayed and volunteered to come along. It was a hard call. In the end there were about fifteen of them, of varying ages and physical condition.

By then Hank had showed up and, as the sheriff had said, he looked pretty tough and in good shape. It was six forty-five and I wanted to be on my way. So I pulled on a rucksack loaded with blankets, soup and coffee. We'd had a captain back in the Regiment who never raised his voice. When he wanted people to listen he spoke quietly, but somehow it made you shut up and listen. I made like him and everyone went quiet.

"My first priority, and yours, is to get to these kids and get them warmed up. I have done this kind of thing before and I know I can get to them in an hour and a half or two at most. I am not going to wait for you. If you can keep up, that's fantastic. If you can't, stay together and keep warm. We have more hot drinks and blankets than we need, so use them and stay safe."

There was a lot of muttering and murmuring as people pulled

on their backpacks, and two minutes later we filed out into the snow and headed unsteadily down the road toward the bridge.

It was slow going and hard work, and it wasn't long before I started to pull ahead. Hank kept pace with me and a couple of the kids even moved ahead for a while. It was still dark, and the snow gave off a strange blue glow which I knew from experience could be dangerously deceptive and lead you far off course, if you did not stick rigidly to what your compass was telling you.

Soon after the bridge we turned north into the forest. According to Hank it was a track, but the only indication of that was the even space between the trees and the strip of clouded sky above our heads. The road itself was buried under a foot or eighteen inches of snow. Where it had drifted against banks and slopes it was up to six feet deep. It was bitterly cold and the condensation from your breath froze on your face and formed into crystals as soon as it left your mouth. We all had scarves over our mouths, or your breath froze on your lips and cracked the skin.

After a while I glanced at Hank. He was doing OK.

"We need to make a decision," I told him, careful to include him in the process. "Some of them are beginning to lag and they need someone to stay with them," he said. "But you need someone to show you the way."

I nodded. "I can't let them slow me down. But we really don't want two groups in need of rescuing."

"So what's on your mind?"

"They're going to need somebody with authority and training if things go wrong."

"Wrong, like what?"

I shrugged. "Like the storm blowing up again, or one of them having a heart attack, or both."

"Wonderful."

"So you stay with them, encourage them to stay warm and keep drinking. Keep the group together. If you get stragglers stop to rest, or go back. I'll take one of the kids to show me the way."

"OK." He squinted at me in the limpid snow-light. "You were special forces, right? Sheriff said you were in Afghanistan."

"Yup."

"SEALs?"

I shook my head. "British Special Air Service. Eight years."

"The SAS? They say they're some tough bastards."

I smiled. "Guy I knew once spent twelve hours lying motionless under just an inch of leaves and topsoil in the jungle, with twenty Colombian cocaine traffickers just thirty paces away. The magazine in his carbine was empty. After twelve hours, when they started packing up their camp, he sat up, smacked in a new magazine and killed every man Jack of them."

I stopped and turned. The group had fallen back. When they saw me turn, they slowly stopped. Their faces said they were praying I'd call a halt.

"OK, guys, I am going to go ahead. Hank is going to stay with you and lead the way. Please remember that snow and extreme cold are treacherous, and you are never more at risk than when you feel comfortable. Keep moving. If you stop, drink something hot and do not stop for too long. If you don't think you can make it, go home. If you die here, you help no one."

I scanned the small crowd. Nobody moved.

"OK, any of the kids here play quarterback? I need the toughest and the strongest one of you to show me the way."

There was a tall, blond kid, probably seventeen or eighteen, standing near the back of the group. He raised his hand. The woman standing next to him, in her early forties, grabbed his arm and muttered something. He ignored her.

"Sir, I'm Mike. I play quarterback. I'm in pretty good shape and I know the way blindfolded. I've done this trek more times than I can remember."

"Let's go, Mike." I beckoned him over and as he approached I addressed the rest of them. "I've been extracted from places where we had to cover not three, but fifteen or twenty miles in frozen mountain conditions, and we've done it. You have two and a half miles to cover, and you can do it if you keep warm and keep moving. We'll see you there."

We turned and I immediately upped the pace. We trudged in silence. Pushing uphill against the soft, yielding snow was exhausting and after another half hour my thighs were aching. The sky was turning gray and dim light was beginning to filter into the air. The snow was easing, with just a few flakes speckling the air. Mike pointed to a large rock on the far side of the snow-covered path, maybe twenty paces ahead.

"That's where we turn off the road and go northeast into the forest. When there's no snow, there's a track you can follow through the trees, but in this light, with the track snowed over, it's going to be hard."

I looked up at the sky. It was going to tell us sweet FA about directions. "Did you bring a compass? I don't usually take one on holiday."

He nodded and smiled. "I brought one."

We crossed the path and moved in among the trees, leaving the boulder on our left. Our pace slowed right down. Not only was the gradient steeper, but we were picking our way, in poor light, among trees and shrubs, and rocks. There was less snow, as most of it had been caught by the canopy, but what there was was turning to ice, slippery and treacherous. That made progress painfully slow.

Mike was a good guide and obviously knew the area well. Though progress was painstaking, and occasionally we strayed off the track, we didn't get lost and at just after eight thirty we finally broke out of the trees on the shores of Stony Lake. The clouds were low and heavy, with dark sagging underbellies. The air coming off the frozen lake was sharp and frigid.

Between where we stood at the tree line and the water's edge there were maybe fifteen or twenty paces. It was hard to tell because the thick blanket of virgin snow seemed to fuse with the sheet of ice on the lake. I looked right and left. The clearing extended for twenty or thirty yards in both directions along the shoreline.

"There's not a footprint nor a tent anywhere in sight," I said.

Mike nodded. "They would have sought cover in among the trees, where they'd be protected from the wind, and the canopy would take most of the snow."

"You've been here with them before. Any idea where they'd go?"

"Maybe." He pointed north, in among the trees. "There's a small clearing about a quarter of a mile, maybe less. They might have gone there to pitch camp."

"Lead the way."

We'd gone a short distance in among the closely packed trees and the snow-laden ferns when, in the dull gray light, something caught my eye.

"Mike, stop, don't move."

He froze and watched me pick my way carefully across the frozen carpet, where it was now more frost than snow. In a space between trees that was wider than the spaces around it, I hunkered down and looked north and then south.

"There is more space between the trees here. Is this a path?"

After a moment he nodded. "Yeah, it could be."

I pointed down at the frozen dusting and a few broken stalks.

"Somebody walked here." I leaned down and gently blew away the most recent snow. Beneath it there was the still visible imprint of a boot. "Size seven or eight, probably a girl. The imprint's not real deep."

I stood and moved down the track a bit. I found another imprint maybe two feet farther back. It was the left foot. I pointed back the way we'd come. "She was going that way. She had one other person with her, maybe, two at most. Which means..." I looked back into the forest, seeing, hearing, feeling nothing. "It means she left the group up ahead of us and she went back to try and find help. So where is she?"

He stared at me, looked in both directions and said, "What do we do now?"

THREE

I STAYED A MOMENT WITHOUT MOVING, HUNKERED down and looking back along the path between the trees.

"We didn't see her tracks when we were coming." I turned to look at Mike. "We didn't see or hear her. Does that path lead anywhere?"

He thought about it for a moment. "Uh, yeah. There's the Jackson Lumber Company. I guess she might have been going there."

I stood. "OK, this could turn into a wild goose chase and we wind up helping nobody. Let's do what we came here to do: Find these people and get these hot drinks and blankets to them. They can tell us how many people went, and where."

We set off at a steady jog through the trees, following the icy track as best we could. It took us a good five minutes, but finally, after several painful falls over hidden, slippery roots, rock and ditches, we came to the clearing.

The tent was not immediately visible. It was at the edge of the clearing and had been partially covered by snow. It looked large enough for four adults at most, but as I looked closer I realized they had draped one tent over another to try and create an air cavity to keep in some of the heat. Then they had packed inside and kept each other warm. It was good, resourceful thinking.

As we approached I could see the snow had been trampled outside the entrance flap, and there were at least two sets of prints leading away, into the woods. Though these had been partially covered by the continuing fall. I raised my voice and shouted, "Anyone here?"

There was some movement, and the flap began to open. A very pale, shivering face peered out and squinted at us. Mike said, "Sam? Is everyone OK?"

"Oh, thank the Lord! We've been praying like crazy!"

She opened the flap fully and clambered out on all fours. She had on a thick, red quilted jacket and ran to Mike to give him an awkward hug. I left them to it and hunkered down in front of the open flap. I could see six people huddled inside, peering out at me. It was hard to tell, with all the quilting and fur, whether they were guys or gals.

"Everybody OK?"

Most of them nodded, but one girl said, "But I don't know how long we would have lasted. Did Suzy call you?"

I opened my rucksack and handed in six flasks of coffee, then handed one up to Sam. I gave them a moment to drink and warm up, then spoke into the dim half-light of the tent again.

"Suzy didn't call us. We saw her tracks back a bit. Where'd she go? Were there two of you with her?"

The girl got on all fours and crawled toward the flap. I stood and helped her out, and gradually, behind her, they all began to stir and make their way out. I took the girl aside to make room and asked her:

"Weren't you at Helen's yesterday, talking to Suzy's parents?"

She smiled with pale blue eyes and freckles. "Yeah, and I wish they'd listened to me. I might have been able to stay in bed this morning." She went up on her toes and shrugged. "Sorry! I guess we were a bit dumb." She held out her hand and we shook. She said, "Rachel."

"Where is Suzy, Rachel? And who's with her?"

"They went to see if there was anyone at the logging company, or if they could call from there. She went with Polly. That was yesterday evening, but they haven't come back yet. I guess they stayed at the mill." She looked embarrassed and added, "I tried to follow, but I couldn't keep up and came back."

I frowned. She looked fit and strong but I didn't pursue it. "How far is it?"

"About half a mile to the fence. The gate's a bit farther on."

"People working there now?"

"I'm not sure. They go pretty quiet from November till April."

I nodded, then addressed them all. "OK, guys. Hot coffee and blankets will help, but what we need here is to start moving and generating heat. I want you all to start packing up your camp. There's a bunch of freezing, shivering parents on their way to rescue you, and you're going to have to help them get home. I want you all to get moving before the weather changes again, and before your parents get much farther from town. I'm going to go and get Suzy and Polly."

"What about me?" It was Mike. "I can show you where it is."

I looked at the others. They had more color in their cheeks and didn't look like they were about to drop dead of hypothermia.

"OK, that'll be a help. Let's get going. We don't have a lot of time before the storm blows up again."

We kept two of the flasks and set off through the wood again, not running this time, but at a brisk walk. We went in silence, billowing clouds of condensation through our scarves. I could feel my toes going numb in my boots, and wondered if Mike was going to be OK. It's not difficult to lose toes to frostbite. All you need to do is ignore the numbness. Pretty soon that toe will die.

Before I could ask him he said, "You think they're OK? It's kind of odd they didn't come back and they didn't call the sheriff."

I gave my head a twitch. "It got pretty wild last night. Smart thing to do would be to stay in the mill. And in that storm, maybe the telephone lines were down. And I'm pretty sure your cells don't work up here."

He laughed a frozen laugh. "No way."

"Your toes OK?"

He nodded. "They'll hold out till the mill. Then I'll give 'em a rub."

Shortly after that we crossed a broad, asphalt road that was largely covered in snow, crossed another four hundred yards of forest and abruptly came out into a broad clearing. There was fifty or sixty paces of open ground and then a tall fence where chicken wire had been attached to tall concrete posts to a height of some ten or twelve feet.

"You know where the entrance is?"

He was hunched into his shoulders. He nodded and jerked his head forward. We tramped on for another hundred yards or so, and pretty soon a large gate became visible up ahead. As we approached I noticed that inside the compound there were signs of one or more vehicles having come in and out through the gate fairly recently—at least during the storm. There were tracks and churned-up sludge which had been protected from the drifting snow by some kind of structure that stood next to the gate. They followed a straight line, out of the gate and along what I gathered was a road that led south and west into the woods.

The gate was made of metal tubing covered in chicken wire, like the fence, and had three large deadbolts, each secured with a hefty padlock. They were all closed and secured. It was impossible to tell whether Suzy and her friend had walked that way. Too much snow had fallen. But leaning on the gate and looking in, I could see that the structure I had noticed was a guard's hut, and beside it was an area of thirty or forty square feet which had been partly protected from the snow. There I could see footprints. Some of them looked pretty small.

Mike said, "Looks like there's no one here."

I studied his face a moment. "There was somebody here, though." I pointed. "See the prints? Two guys, pretty big. One has tractor tires, the other straight ridges. And two girls. The gate's closed, but trucks have been in and out since the snow started. You can see that by the tracks and the dirty sludge beside the hut."

He stared at me. He was beginning to look worried. "Maybe they got a ride into town?"

"Maybe. How well do you know Suzy and Polly?"

"Pretty well."

"Are they the kind of girls who would get a ride in a truck, leaving all their friends to sit out the storm, just half a mile away?" He didn't say anything. He just looked queasy. I said, "I didn't think so."

I stood a moment, uncertain what to do, then asked him, "If I follow this road, where the truck went, I will eventually come to the big rock, right, where we turned off into the forest."

"Yeah, after about a mile or so, I guess."

"OK, I want you to go back with the group. When you meet up with them, I want you to go back and tell the sheriff I am following the road from the mill, and I am looking for Suzy and Polly. I am going to need him and his deputies out here with trucks and first aid, soon. Those girls could be in serious trouble. You got that?"

"Yes, sir."

He turned and headed back at an unsteady jog that must have really hurt his feet. I had another look through the gate and the fence, wondering if I had read the signs wrong. But I was pretty sure I hadn't. They had got inside the gate, and shortly after that they had got into a truck, willingly or unwillingly.

I turned and started tramping down the road, following the dirty tracks of the truck. By the width and depth of those tracks I figured it was at least a seven-ton vehicle, maybe bigger. That meant they had a large, warm, comfortable cab, possibly with a sleeping compartment.

The thought made me break into what was called the Rifleman's March, where you walk ten paces and run ten paces, walk ten paces run ten paces. It's a great way of covering ground at speed, and it also keeps you warm.

After sixty yards the road entered deep forest and then described a big loop to the right. The tracks here were clear and easy to follow, as the road had been partially protected from the snowfall by the trees, and there had been no other traffic. After about fifteen or twenty minutes I came to what I had been expecting, and dreading. The tracks veered toward the side of the road, and there, much of the snow had melted into a large pool of dirty sludge, where it had frozen. The truck had pulled over and parked.

I approached carefully, staying out on the dusted, slippery blacktop. It was easy to see where the cab had been, because that was where the heat from the engine had melted the snow. And on the far side, on the verge, the frozen grass had been trodden down and trampled. From that point there was a series of scrambled prints leading in among the trees. From what I could make out they were large boots, and only two sets of tracks.

There was a hollow pit in my gut as I picked my way in among the glazed ferns and the trees, keeping a couple of feet or three away from the tracks so as not to disturb them. The tracks were uneven and looked unsteady. A couple of times I came across areas where it was clear a foot had slipped and scraped, and somebody had fallen, crushing ferns and squashing the snow beneath.

It was hard to be sure, with the steady fall of snow and the freezing conditions, but the two guys walking into the woods seemed to have caused a lot more havoc than you'd expect, unless they were falling down drunk.

Or unless they were carrying something heavy.

A couple of minutes later I confirmed they had been carrying something heavy.

They still had horror frozen onto their expressions. Their hoods had been pulled back from their heads. Their faces were waxy pale, with bulging eyes, and their clothes were ripped in various places. I recognized Suzy straight away, but it was weird because it wasn't Suzy anymore. She had been a sweet, brave kid, with a lot of spirit and personality. There was a heat in my belly, rage stifled by grief and impotence. This was irreversible. This was not something you could fix before her parents saw it. She had been destroyed. Completely and irretrievably. She was sitting, with her legs straight out in front of her, propped against a tree. Next to her was Polly.

I recognize Polly from Helen's Family Restaurant too. She was lying on her belly, with her arms and legs at odd, uncomfortable angles and her face turned toward me. She looked terrified, but I knew she wasn't. There was no feeling in her at all. Her heart and her mind were still. I saw a snowflake rest gently on her eye, and half expected her to blink. But she felt nothing. She was nothing.

I turned and headed back toward the road, kicking away the snow to mark a clear path for the sheriff to follow when he got there. Back at the road I picked up branches and rocks from where I could find them and sectioned off the area where the truck had parked, and the entrance to the path. It took me a good fifteen minutes, and when I was done I sat on my rucksack and drank some hot coffee.

Before long I began to hear voices, and after a while, down the road, I saw the seven kids and their parents making their way toward us. I have faced death—my own death and others'—a hundred times, but I have never felt such dread as I felt in that moment, seeing Emma in that crowd, raising her hand to wave to me.

It took them a good two or three minutes to draw close. I stood as they approached and moved toward them. I could see Emma's eyes flitting over the scene behind me, taking in the branches and the rocks. She smiled at me, as though, if we all kept being normal and polite to each other, nothing really bad could happen.

"Did you find Suzy and Polly?" she asked. Hank was pointing. "What's with the branches and the stones, Mr. Bauer?"

I raised both hands.

"We haven't much time, and we are moving very slow. The storm could be on us again in a couple of hours. So I need you all to hurry home, back to town, and as soon as you can," I turned to Hank, "I need you to send the sheriff out here with a truck and, if you have one, a snow plow."

Emma was shaking her head, frowning at me and then looking past me at the melted stones and the branches. "No," she was saying, "No, wait. What has happened? What is all this you've done here? You need to tell me what has happened!"

I grabbed her hand and pulled her toward me. "Emma! We have no time for this! You need to keep moving back toward town."

Her eyes were suddenly wild. She wrenched her hand free and pointed. "Is Suzy in there! Answer me! Is Suzy in there?"

"I don't know," I lied. "There are tracks, I can't follow them alone."

"Tracks? *Tracks?* Why? Why would Suzy and Polly go in there? You are *lying! What have you done to my daughter?*"

I took a hold of her, saying, "Now take it easy, take it easy." I was making faces at Hank, shaking my head and saying, "We just haven't got time for this. You need to get going, *now*, and send me the sheriff." I turned to Emma and stared her straight in the eyes. "Emma! Emma, listen to me! I don't know where Suzy is. OK? I have not found her. But there are tracks we need to follow. Now, go home!"

To Hank I said, "Get me the sheriff and any other deputies you have. Tell them it is very urgent."

As he hurried ahead of the group I looked up at the darkening, gunmetal sky. The temperature was dropping and the wind was picking up, dragging frozen ghosts across the road.

If the sheriff didn't come and get me, in a few hours I might be one of those ghosts myself.

FOUR

As it was he showed up with Hank about ten minutes later in a Ford pickup. He pulled up beside the patch of melted snow, which was steadily disappearing under the fresh fall, climbed out of his truck and stood staring at it.

"What is this, Mr. Bauer? Are you trying to cause trouble?"

I wiped the flakes from my face and my eyes and muttered, "I'm trying to save you some trouble, Sheriff." I pointed back the way I had come. "I followed these tracks from the Jackson sawmill. They stopped here. You can still just about see the dirty, melted sludge where the truck was parked with the engine running. I've marked it off and I've taken some pictures, but it won't be visible much longer."

I turned and pointed into the woods. "I followed a couple of sets of tracks into the forest. Two large men. You'd better come and see for yourself."

I led the way in among the trees and ferns, pointing to my right as we went.

"Those are the tracks they made. You can see they were clumsy and fell a few times."

Hank muttered, "Were they drunk or what?" but he didn't sound very convinced. I didn't answer straight away. I said,

"No...," but when we eventually came to the spot I pointed to the two girls. "They were carrying Suzy and Polly."

You don't often hear people truly gasp. But Hank gasped, a sharp intake of breath. I looked at him and he had his hands over his mouth. Sheriff Davies had turned away. "Oh, my God," he whispered, then covered his face and began to sob.

You grow hard in the city. They talk about community, but it's impersonal. City communities are made of institutions, institutionalized care and statutory compassion. In places like this, the community was an organic, living thing where people cared because they knew each other.

I said, "I'm sorry."

He gave his head a single shake and wiped his eyes on his sleeve. "I was at their christenings. I've known them..." But he couldn't go on. His lip curled in and he walked away, with his back to us, breathing great plumes of condensation. I turned to Hank. He was weeping too.

"We need to get the ME here, we need crime scene officers, and we need to get these bodies to the morgue."

"That's Suzy, and Polly." He said it like I'd got their names wrong. Then, "ME's in Machias. She ain't gonna be able to get here for a day, at least. Maybe more."

I heard a snuffle and a footfall. The sheriff was wiping his face again, looking at the two bodies.

"This ain't New York, Mr. Bauer. We don't have murders out here. We don't have crime officers just a phone call away. Crime techs would have to come in from Augusta. That's a hundred and fifty miles away. In this weather it could be days, maybe a week. We ain't a big priority for them." He gave me a curious look. "You a cop?" I shook my head, but he insisted. "But you got some involvement, I can tell. This kind of thing ain't new to you."

He was watching me carefully and I knew I had to say something. So I told him something like the truth.

"I'm involved in private security. When I was with the Regiment we did a lot of covert, undercover operations. You learn a few things. You've got a competent doctor?"

They looked at each other. We were all beginning to shiver. The temperature was dropping fast. Hank said, "Doc Johansen. He's a good doctor."

I pulled my cell and took several photographs of the scene, saying, "In these conditions the ground is going to tell us practically nothing. Sheriff, why don't you and I get the bodies to the truck while Hank gets photographs of the tracks and the melted snow on the road? You got some tarps in the pickup?"

It was a gruesome job, made worse because we kept slipping and falling, and the bodies, frozen solid by the plummeting temperatures, clattered and clunked when they hit the ground.

We finally got them into the back of the truck, covered them in the tarpaulins, clambered in, shivering, and made our way slowly and carefully back to town.

The morgue was beside the sheriff's office. Sheriff Davies had radioed ahead so Dr. Johansen was there to meet us and help get the bodies inside. He was a tall, willowy man in his sixties, with a shock of white hair swept back from his face and an expression that said he'd seen a hundred dead bodies, but never thought he'd live to see these particular ones.

When he had them set awkwardly on the tables, the three of them just stood staring, like they were trying to work out some terrible puzzle. The girls didn't seem human, frozen as they were into bizarre positions: one sitting, the other with her limbs twisted.

The sheriff shook his head. "I can't..." He looked at me. "I'm going to talk to Emma and Ned, and Polly's parents." He swallowed and looked away. "I don't know what I'm going to tell them. I know you meant well," he turned back to me, "but when the weather improves, if I was you, I'd move on to Jonesboro or Addison."

I arched an eyebrow at him. "Thanks for the advice. Nothing like encouraging a civic spirit."

"You told that woman you didn't know where her daughter was."

"As it was we barely got those people out of there on time. Can you imagine what she would have done if she'd known her daughter's body was in those woods? Can you imagine what it would have done to her to see her daughter like that?"

He sighed and rubbed his face. "I know."

"The poor damn woman has been through enough. Just tell her we went into the forest and found the bodies. And for Christ's sake give them time to thaw out before their parents see them. They can't see their daughters like this."

He nodded. "I'll see you in the morning."

He left and I turned to the doc, who was cautiously examining the bodies.

"Can you determine cause of death?"

"Not like this."

"When they thaw."

Hank winced at the term, but the doc shrugged. "Probably." He approached Polly and fingered her clothes. "We'll have to get these off, see if they sustained any injuries. There was no blood at the scene?"

"No, but they might have been killed at the mill or in the truck." I pointed at Suzy's neck. "There is a lot of bruising on her neck, but her face is not bloated. The tongue, the eyes..." I shook my head.

"No, I wouldn't say she was strangled. But her neck may have been broken. We'll have to wait and see."

"How about fingerprints? You can get them from the neck, right?"

He and Hank looked at each other, then Hank said, "I guess."

I sighed. "You can, skin holds a print extremely well. But you want to get them before the skin on their necks thaws out." Nobody moved. I raised my eyebrows at Hank. He swallowed. "Me?"

"Yeah, Hank. You're the cops, remember?"

He left to get the fingerprinting equipment. He thought he remembered where it was. As the door banged behind him I studied the doctor's face. He studied mine back. We were both thinking the same thing. I said it.

"Who rapes a woman in the snow, then puts her clothes back on?"

He shook his head. "I am not a forensic pathologist, Mr. Bauer." He paused a moment, then went on. "Though I agree, it seems odd."

"They were in that much of a hurry to dispose of them, they dumped them practically by the side of the road, making no effort to conceal their tracks," I pointed at the girls' clothes, "but they took the time and trouble to put their clothes back on?" I smiled. "You don't need to be a forensic pathologist to see that."

He gave a heavy sigh and looked down at the floor.

"Mr. Bauer, I don't know what you want me to say. When the bodies have thawed out a little I'll be able to determine cause of death, I hope. And I can check to see if they have been raped, but other than that there isn't a lot we can do." He paused, raised his eyes to meet mine. "You should also be aware that the telephone lines are down, and so is the internet. We are not going to be getting help any time soon."

I heard the outer door bang and a gust of cold air moved the swing doors of the morgue. I made to move, but paused and frowned.

"This mill—"

"The Jackson Lumber Company up by the lake."

"Yeah, does it belong to somebody in Balthazar?"

He shook his head. "No, I don't think so. The fact is I don't know. I think it's a Canadian company."

"So those boys are on their way to Canada right now."

"More than likely."

I thanked him and moved toward the door as Hank came in stamping and clapping his hands. He had a small attaché case with him. I took hold of the door but before leaving I said, "Will you keep me in the loop, Doc?"

He suppressed a scowl. "Is there any reason I should?"

"Yeah, because I was willing to risk my life to save seven of your kids, and the two I couldn't save were murdered. I'd like to know who by."

He was quiet for a moment. Then, "I'm sorry. We must seem ungrateful."

I nodded. "Yeah. You could say that. I'll drop in tomorrow."

Hank stopped me. "Mr. Bauer?"

"What?"

"Thanks. I guess we're all a bit shook up. This kind of thing don't happen here. But thanks."

I nodded and left.

It was mid-afternoon, but by the time I got outside it was almost as dark as night. The sky was bellying low with heavy ash and charcoal clouds. When I reached the corner, intending to turn toward my rental house on the right, through the trees on my left I saw the lights of Helen's Family Restaurant burning a warm amber among all the cold gray. They looked inviting, and, on an impulse, I turned and trudged toward them.

It was warm inside. The place was empty but for Helen who was checking her register roll. She glanced at me and smiled, then started counting louder so I'd know not to interrupt her. I climbed on a stool and waited. When she was done and had made a note she said, "Hi, handsome. What's cooking?" Before I could answer she narrowed her eyes. "You OK? You look rough."

"You haven't heard? I thought news traveled fast in small towns."

"Not when there's a snowstorm on."

"Yeah, I didn't expect you to be open."

"Bit of snow don't scare me. What can I get you?"

"I could use some hot coffee laced with whiskey, and maybe a couple of burgers."

“Coming right up.” She spoke while she poured. “So what haven’t I heard?”

“Suzy, and a friend of hers called Polly—” I paused because she’d gone pale as she handed me my cup. “I’m sorry,” I said, “they were found…” I sighed. “I found them. We organized a group to go help the kids who’d been trapped up by the lake. It turned out Suzy and Polly had gone to try and get help from the sawmill. I went to look for them.”

She had frozen, listening. Now she said, “You said ‘found.’ Are they OK?”

“No. They’re dead.”

She put her hands to her mouth in a strange echo of Hank’s gesture. “Oh, my God! But they were so young and healthy! Surely…”

“They didn’t die of cold, Helen. They were murdered.”

She put a hand on the counter. Her eyes swiveled left and right, like she was searching for logic and common sense. Finally she met my eye and shook her head.

“No. That doesn’t… It doesn’t make any sense. I mean, *here?* Who?”

“Couple of workers from the mill. I followed the girls’ tracks to the logging company. When they got there they were picked up in a truck at the gate. The truck drove down, south, probably headed for Route 86, going to Canada. It stopped after about half a mile. You could see where the tracks pulled off the road.”

I paused and sipped the coffee. There was a generous shot of bourbon in it, so I took another and set the cup down.

“They had left a pretty clear trail. They were clumsy and they kept falling in the snow. They just left the bodies there, under the trees.”

She pulled over a stool from the cash register and climbed on it. “Those bastards. I’d castrate them, I sweat to God, then hang ’em high. Those poor kids. How…?”

“I don’t know yet. They were frozen,”

She winced. “So they were there a long time.”

"At least a few hours, I guess. They had bruising on their necks."

"Were they raped?"

"Maybe, can't tell yet. They were fully dressed. So it seems unlikely. To me, at least."

She became abstracted. "So maybe they were raped at the mill. They got dressed and then they were driven to the forest. Or they were raped while they were in the truck, then they got dressed..." She trailed off.

I shrugged. "It would make more sense to kill them at the mill, after raping them. Less chance of being caught. Who knows? None of it makes much sense. What do you know about the mill?"

"Are you a policeman?"

"No. Why does everybody keep asking me that?"

"You have that law enforcement air about you. I'm going to put your burgers on. You must be starving."

She got up and I pushed my cup across to her. "Fix me another one of these, will you?"

She disappeared in back and after a moment I heard the hiss of frozen burgers being dropped onto a hot griddle. That was followed a couple of minutes later by the smell of frying onions. Then she came out and leaned with her forearm on the doorjamb.

"I don't know anything about the mill," she said, answering my earlier question. "Except it's been there as long as the village. It was founded by Balthazar Jones back in the day. Then it was bought by some Canadian."

"The workers must come into town to do their shopping, have drinks..."

She shook her head and pulled the corners of her mouth down. "No. I never really thought about it till now. Fact is they keep to themselves. Maybe one or two have come in and had a coffee, but I wouldn't be able to tell you. I don't know them by sight."

"Who owns the mill?"

She went back into the kitchen. There was more hissing and after a moment she reappeared.

"I don't know," she said. "Like I said, I heard some Canadian bought it years ago. I mean, it's what, twenty, thirty miles to St. Stephen at the border? I guess I just figured they did all their business north of the border."

I grunted. "Well, this was some business they did south of the border."

She brought me my burgers and we sat in silence while I ate. When I drained my coffee and was wiping my mouth on a paper napkin, she suddenly gave a rueful smile.

"I guess you'll be moving on now, huh?"

"That was the sheriff's advice. He didn't think I'd be too popular after this."

"That's bullshit. People ain't that stupid. We all know you were trying to help."

I frowned. "How come he's not at the county seat? Shouldn't he be in Machias?"

"Yeah, but he was born and raised here, and it's just six miles. So he kind of goes back and forth."

"Now he's stuck here."

"Till the storm blows over, yeah."

I looked over at the window, where the flakes were falling steadily in a dark, gray street. It felt like the storm would never blow over.

FIVE

We talked for half an hour while I had a whiskey and warmed up. Finally I paid and stood to go, but as I climbed off the stool I saw a shadow move outside and the door burst inward, allowing in a gust of wind and a swirl of snow, and with it Emma, Suzy's mother.

She stood a moment staring at me, then let go the door and it swung closed, muffling the sound of the wind. Her face was distorted and her cheeks were wet with tears. She hadn't bothered to do up her quilted coat and her pullover was speckled with snow. Her mouth moved but no sound came out.

I said, "Emma, I am so sorry..." but ran out of words.

She took a couple of steps forward, reaching for me. Her face was twisted with pain. "Is it true?"

"Yes..."

She shook her head in rapid jerks, telling me I had misunderstood the question. "Is it true you're a soldier?"

I frowned. "Yes."

She stared at my chest, her eyes flitting this way and that like she was looking for something there. She put her hands on me and I held her elbows. Her eyes came back to my face and there was craziness in them.

"Is it true you were special forces?"

"Yes. Listen, you'd better sit down."

I sat her at the nearest table and Helen brought over a pot of coffee and three cups. Emma ignored her and gripped my hand.

"Find them," she hissed. "Find them and punish them."

I held her hand in both of mine. "That's what the sheriff is going to do, Emma. I'll help in any way I can—"

She began sobbing, big, ugly convulsive sobs. "He won't! He won't do it!"

I turned to Helen. "Maybe get her a brandy, or a whiskey?" She nodded and left to fetch a drink. I squeezed Emma's hands and spoke quietly. "I want you to listen to me, Emma. I know what you're going through, and I know it feels like the pain is never going to stop. And in some ways that is true. But it's also true that you learn to live with it. And you'll find ways of keeping her close. But I promise you, the sheriff and the cops are going to do everything they can..."

I trailed off because she was shaking her head again, and she said very quietly, "He's *not*."

I asked, equally quietly, "What makes you say that?"

She took a deep breath. Helen returned with a bottle of bourbon and poured Emma a stiff shot. Emma took hold of the glass and considered it a moment before draining it. She shuddered and met my eye.

"Because he told me you think it was murder, but he doesn't agree. He says they wandered off looking for help, got lost in the snow and the woods and died of hypothermia. He says ever since you arrived you have been trying to stir up trouble, scaremongering and trying to be the center of attention. So, believe me, he is not going to investigate."

I scowled, then turned to Helen.

"Why would he do that? The medical report will show—"

Helen interrupted. "Maybe it will and maybe it won't. Walt is up for reelection soon, and he wants to be seen as the big daddy who makes sure nothing bad ever happens in his burg. A murder committed in his hometown, by workers at the sawmill...?" She shook her head. "That sawmill's been there for years. It won't look good for him."

Emma still had my hands in hers and clutched them tight. "You have skills, you know things. Walt said you knew about police procedure and investigation. You found her. You have to do it. I'll pay you anything. I'll sell the house. Whatever you want. But you hunt those bastards down and you *punish* them!"

I shook my head again. "He can't do that. The evidence..."

"Evidence my ass!" It was Helen again. "What little evidence you have is gonna be buried in snow by morning, and in a week it will have melted away."

"The medical report!"

"The medical report will say whatever Walt wants it to say. Doc Johansen is a good man, but if Walt leans on him he'll put whatever Walt says on the death certificate."

I scowled at her. "*Why?*"

Emma spoke quietly, looking down at a wet handkerchief in her hands. "Walt is the doctor's brother-in-law. The doctor has no family, aside from Walt's sister, who is much younger than he is. You don't get a lot of choice up here. Anyhow, after Walt's father died a couple of years ago, he became like the patriarch, and what he says goes, in his family and in the town."

I leaned back in my chair. "What about the mayor? You must have a mayor we can talk to, or is he Walt's brother-in-law too?"

They looked at each other. Helen sighed and looked embarrassed. "The mayor is Walt's uncle. We vote for him because he's always been the mayor and we all love him. But really, it's Walt who makes all the decisions. And..." She shrugged and they both glanced at each other and shrugged together. "Most of the time..."

And Emma interjected, "Most of the time he does a pretty good job."

I rubbed my face and ran my fingers through my hair. "I am having trouble believing the sheriff would suppress evidence of a murder, of two young girls from his own hometown, just to ensure his reelection. I mean, the guy is a bit of a jerk, but..." I ran out of words and went with, "Besides, from what you say he has everything sewn up here!"

Emma blew her nose. "Sure, in Balthazar, but he has the whole county to think of. And believe me, there are plenty of people in Machias who complain he spends too much time in his hometown and he neglects the rest of the county. They would just welcome the opportunity to throw this in his face. 'Can't even keep his own house in order, how can he expect to look after the county?'"

Helen nodded. "That's it, plus, I know Walt, and he won't think of it as suppressing evidence. No sir, what he will do is convince himself they were not murdered...," they both looked at each other, nodding and speaking at the same time, "...that it was *their* fault!"

Emma said, "Exactly! He'll blame them for being irresponsible and not listening to his advice—"

"And so making himself look good!"

"And he'll blame you," she pointed at me, "for trying to stir up trouble in his town."

We sat in silence for a moment. In spite of my better judgment, my mind was already off working out how I would do it, what the unknown quantities were and what equipment I would need. I drummed the table with my fingers.

"When you say punish..."

Her face went as hard as ice. She said, "Old Testament."

I nodded. "But you leave everything to me."

Her face grew fierce. "They killed my *daughter!* I want proof! I want to *see* it!"

I leaned forward, took her hands again and looked hard into her eyes. "I know what it is to kill a person, Emma. It changes you. It destroys you inside and you become irreparable. Nobody can ever fix you after that. I will give you your satisfaction, but you let me do the job. You will walk away from this, you'll go back to your husband, to your family, knowing justice has been done, and there will be some healing. But only if you let me do the job."

She was quiet for a long time. Finally she said, "How much is this going to cost?"

"That's the price," I said, "that you go back to your husband and your family with clean hands."

Tears welled in her eyes again. She put her elbows on the table, buried her face in her hands and began to sob. Just then the door opened. There was a moment while the wind tried to suck it closed again, then there was a billow of snow and Sheriff Walt Davies stepped in, stamping his boots and beating the snow from his hat. He stood a moment watching us with little expression on his face.

I said, "Sheriff," and Helen got up to go get some hot coffee. Emma remained with her face in her hands.

"I thought I told you to stay at home, Emma. What's Ned doing, letting you go out alone on a night like this, the way you're feeling?"

I answered for her, and his face said he didn't like that.

"She came to ask me why I had lied, and to tell her exactly what I had found. I told her the girls had probably lost their way. It's an easy thing to do in a forest when there's heavy snow. You lose all sense of direction. Hypothermia can come on suddenly if your core temperature drops, and that makes you sleepy. You sit down to rest and fall asleep. Sometimes you get a rupturing of blood vessels in the skin, which can give the impression of bruising, but it is just a reaction to the extreme cold. Either way, it is the most peaceful way to die." I spread my hands. "She needed closure, Sheriff. She found me here."

She said, in a wet, nasally voice, "I tried the morgue, I tried Mr. Bauer's house, and finally I saw the lights on here. So I came in."

He looked down at the floor and chewed his lip for a moment. Finally he said, "Well, you found what you came for, Emma. Now you got your husband and two young kids waiting for you at home. It's time to go back."

She didn't move, but her eyes rose and fastened on mine. "Thank you, Mr. Bauer. I do feel better after what you have explained to me."

She stood and made her way to where the sheriff stood. He put an arm around her and guided her to the door. There he paused and looked at me for a long moment. His expression was hard to read. After a moment he nodded once and said, "Thanks." Then they both stepped out into the dark and the cold.

Helen was leaning on the counter with the jug of hot coffee in her hand. When he'd gone she said, "Boy, life sucks sometimes, don' it?"

I nodded a few times, then offered her the kind of smile you'd call rueful. "It do. What about you, Helen?"

"What kind of a question is that? What about me? Do I suck?"

I laughed. "Family? Kids? Husband?"

"You want to know if I am married? Am I available?"

She brought the coffee around the counter and sat opposite me at the table. I asked, "Is that a bad thing?"

"Well," she poured us both more coffee and laced it, "considering you only just arrived and you brought with you a crazy snowstorm and two murders..." She closed her eyes. "Sorry, that's not fair. There was you looking for a rest and a holiday..." She frowned suddenly at her cup. "You ain't really going to do that, are you?"

"Do what?"

"Find those boys and..." She trailed off.

"Kill them?" She nodded. I didn't answer straight away. When I did I said, "That's two questions. Am I going to hunt them down and find them? And am I going to kill them when I do?"

"And?"

"Yes, I am going to hunt them down and find them. But I am

not a murderer, Helen." I smiled and her cheeks colored. "For me to take justice into my own hands," I went on, "it would have to be something pretty extreme."

"Like what? What does that mean? Murdering two young girls isn't extreme enough for you?"

I made a face like I had never really thought about it till then. "Of course it's extreme. But that is what cops and the whole legal system is for. For me to go out and kill someone, I don't know, it would have to be something like crimes against humanity, Putin, Saddam Hussein, the Ayatollahs. That kind of thing."

"So raping and murdering two girls from some village in Maine ain't as bad as what Putin and Saddam and all those guys did?"

"Are you trying to pick a fight with me, Helen?" I smiled. "In the first place we don't know yet whether they were raped. It seems unlikely. And in the second place, I said I was going to find them and bring them in—"

"You said you were going to hunt them down and punish them. And you made Emma promise she would leave it to you. I'm starting to think maybe you're a pussy. If you can't finish the job, boy, you bring 'em to me and I'll put a bullet through their goddamn heads!"

She wasn't smiling. She meant it. I said, "You're not from New England, are you?"

"Wyoming. I married a man from Maine because he was sweet and gentle."

"What happened?"

"He died. See? In Wyoming, a man don't do that. In Wyoming, a man says he's gonna do something, and he does it. He don't chicken out with chickenshit excuses."

"You made your point, Helen."

"You can't let that woman down, Harry."

"I don't plan to."

"Well, if you bring those boys in and hand them over to the sheriff..."

The look in my eye stopped her. After a moment I said quietly, "I don't plan to."

"OK." She smiled. Then after a moment she laughed. "You know what we call a Texan gun collection back in Wyoming?"

"Are you missing home, Helen? Tell me, what do you call a Texan gun collection?"

"A kiddy's starter pack!"

She hooted and fell about laughing. I smiled and when she was done I said, "I'm going to need some kind of vehicle that will get me through the snow and up to the sawmill. Any ideas?"

She watched me a while, with half a smile. "I'll give it some thought. If you took the Old Vicarage Road, that goes mostly through pretty dense forest, so there might be less snow on the road. I've got an old army Land Rover which will get through most anything." Her smile deepened. "I also got a snowmobile I could lend you."

I narrowed my eyes at her. "You have a snowmobile? I could have used that this morning!"

"You should've asked. If I'd known you were going I would have offered!"

"The sheriff might have mentioned it."

"He don't know I have it. What he don't know, they can't tax." She winked. "So here's what I'm thinking. You had lunch about four."

"OK."

"So what time were you figuring on having dinner?"

"I hadn't really thought about it. Why?"

"See, my house is on the other side of the river, just by the Old Vicarage Road. Now, I'm thinking you must be all tuckered out after what you done this morning. So why don't you come home with me, I'll cook your supper, you can have some of my blueberry pie, and then you can go for a drive on my snowmobile."

"I thought blueberries were in the summer."

A touch of compassion entered her eyes. "That's what the freezer is for, honey."

"Well, that sounds like quite a plan. I don't think I can say no."

She winked. "Nobody ever said no to me before, and you ain't gonna be the first."

I stood and looked down at her. "There's just one thing I want you to do for me."

"Name it."

She stood and I pulled her to me. "Whisper 'y'all' in my ear, like a cowgirl."

SIX

By the time we'd finished with the blueberry pie it was three in the morning. I put on several layers of clothes and we pushed the snowmobile out of the garage. While we were at it I borrowed a few tools I thought might come in handy, including some wire cutters and a flashlight.

Helen's house was over the river, on the north side where there was just a scattering of houses, and her nearest neighbors were a few hundred yards away. So I was unlikely to be seen by anyone, even if they heard the snowmobile. She had drawn me a map, which I had memorized, but in any case, she told me, I could not miss it.

"You just follow the road. You are going to see a broad line of snow between the trees. Stay on it and you'll be on the road. In two hundred and fifty yards you're gonna turn left, and you're gonna go a quarter of a mile north. Almost at the end you're gonna see Rosie's place, the old vicarage, on your right. Go past that and pretty soon you gonna turn right. Then you go straight for half a mile and you'll find you're on the road where you found Suzy and Polly. From there on in you know the way."

As I swung my leg over and climbed astride the machine, she'd gripped my arm and said, "Just one more thing."

Then she'd handed me a Smith and Wesson 29 and a box of rounds. "It belonged to my daddy," she'd said. "Look after it." She'd given me a kiss and at three twenty sharp I had accelerated away into the dark, with the strange, luminous snow all around me, enhancing the blackness. Progress was fast and, pretty soon, as she had said I turned left, following the gap between the trees which, when there was no snow, was a road.

Here, after the left turn, the trees closed in and the gap grew narrower. The snow over the blacktop was not so thick, only a foot or two, and I began to worry that I might start biting into the asphalt. I kept going and pretty soon I came to a bend to the right where the snow grew deeper. I slowed and, and as I took the bend I saw, over on my right, a tall, austere house set back from the road, and, barely visible in the light from the snowmobile, the shadow of a tall church spire.

I paused long enough for a quick look, then sped on. Five minutes later I came to the big bend in the road where the truck had stopped and melted the snow. I kept going and a couple of minutes after that I came to the clearing beyond which was the sawmill. I stopped, killed the lights and the engine and sat motionless. It was icy cold. Looking up, it was as though there were no sky. You felt you could reach up and touch the ceiling of clouds. The wind was not a gale, but it moaned and whistled in the tall pines. I gave it a full minute and didn't see a glimmer of light or of movement at the mill.

It was two or three hundred yards to the gate, and for a moment I debated whether to walk or ride. Time was of the essence and a quick getaway might be crucial. The noise of the snowmobile made it a risk, but everything was a risk and the bottom line was, I wanted to have the vehicle to hand if I needed it. So I took it easy and rode to within thirty paces of the entrance. Through the chicken-wire fence I saw nothing: no lights, no movement, nothing but darkness and stillness. So I killed the engine and the lights again and pulled Helen's wire cutters from my pocket.

Fortunately they had rubber handles, because when I touched the fence, sparks buzzed, flashed and crackled. I waited, watching and listening. Still nothing but the moan of the wind in the trees. So I took the cutters and clipped a six-foot, vertical cut in the fence, then cut across four feet and made a big upside-down L. If I needed to make a quick escape, there was no sense scrambling through a two-foot hole at ground level.

I folded back the flap and eased through.

On my right there wasn't much to see except for the dark bulks of large stacks of timber, twelve or fifteen feet high. On my left I could make out the dark form of the guard's hut by the gate, where I had seen the tracks and the footprints the day before, and about thirty paces opposite that, a collection of large, black shadows, darker than the darkness, which I knew to be a complex of wooden buildings. After another few seconds wait I loped toward those hulking shadows across the snow.

When I got there I pressed up against the clapboard wall and peered around the corner. I could just make out a courtyard enclosed by three sets of two- and three-story buildings forming a kind of U. I could see windows, black panes of glass with nothing behind them.

The nearest door was about two feet to my right, around the corner I was leaning against. I figured it was as good a place as any to start, so I slipped around, spent a couple of minutes applying my Swiss Army knife with numb fingers, and finally heard the latch open. The door swung in and I followed it, closing the door behind me.

There were two windows beside the door. Now I was on the inside, there was an eerie luminescence to the courtyard outside. The snow, on the ground and on the roofs, had a strange, blue glow that partially illuminated the room.

The floors were bare boards. The walls were bare wood and the roof was more wood laid across wooden rafters. I guessed it was what you'd expect from a logging company sawmill.

Down the center of the room, which was probably thirty feet

long and fifteen feet wide, there was a long table with fifteen or more chairs set either side of it. It was hard to tell the exact number in the poor light. I walked around the room, but there was little more to see aside from a small kitchen which came off the far end.

It was dark inside. There were no windows, so I clicked on the flashlight Helen had given me and played the luminous circle around the small room. It was about nine foot square, with an ancient stove with a big aluminum pot on it, an even more ancient fridge, a sink piled high with dirty dishes.

I thought that was interesting. A table big enough for thirty people, and a kitchen where the washing up was left for later. I peered inside the pot. There had been a stew there. I could make out a green been, a small piece of what was either beef or pork, and some thick, brown liquid. There was no mold. So they had been there recently, and they had left before anyone had had time to wash the dishes.

A door in the back wall opened onto a wooden staircase. I climbed the stairs, increasingly certain the whole place had been abandoned. Another door at the top opened onto a room as long as the dining room downstairs. Windows in the wall allowed in enough light to show a row of beds. They had all been slept in, but nobody had bothered to make them afterwards.

I played the flashlight across the floor. The cold, damp weather had preserved the wet footprints: small prints. There were lots of them, too many to count, all merging with each other.

I went down and examined the floor in the dining room. It was the same.

A sudden flash of impatience made me wrench open the door, not caring if I was heard or seen, and step out into the yard. I glanced at the building on my right, the bottom of the U, but decided the building opposite was nearer. I crossed and instead of fiddling with the lock I kicked the door in and went inside.

It was wider than the other building, and longer. It was a

workshop, like a long barn, littered with benches, saws, a variety of other tools and large stacks of timber. There were no wet floors here. I left it and crossed to the remaining building. I kicked that door in too and stepped into an office. There was a desk and a phone directly in front of the door, and to the left an open space with a couple of vinyl armchairs, a melamine table and an ashtray. No computer. The floor showed a few damp marks, but not much, and what prints I could make out looked like big boots. I followed them with the beam from the flashlight. An open archway led to a staircase. An indefinable sense of menace had made me pull the Smith and Wesson from my pocket. I climbed the stairs with the weapon held out in front of me and found myself on a landing with several offices branching off ahead, right and left.

The first two I went into were empty. The third was fully equipped with filing cabinets, a desk, a computer and a photocopier. There was also an old iron safe in the corner.

I sat at the desk and opened a couple of drawers. There was nothing much in there, paperclips, staples, a couple of pens. I stood and, using my Swiss Army knife, prized open the top drawer of the old filing cabinet. Unsurprisingly, it was full of files. I grabbed a fistful and took them over to the desk. I opened the first one and frowned at the first page. Then I skipped to the third and the eighth, and frowned at them too.

A squeak of timber made me switch off the flashlight and rise silently from the desk to go and stand by the open door. There was nobody on the landing, but another soft creak told me someone was climbing the stairs, trying not to be heard.

I switched on the flashlight again, set it on the desk pointed at the open door and stepped outside, leaving the door ajar. Then I hunkered down in the shadows. Thirty seconds later a figure appeared at the top of the stairs. He'd had the sense to switch his own flashlight off, but his form was visible in the faint glow from the window. He could see the light from the flashlight and very slowly took three cautious steps toward it. Now, by the light of the flashlight, I could see he had a semi-automatic in his right hand. With his left he pushed the door open and stepped inside.

I knew I had four seconds while he processed the unexpected situation. I didn't waste any of them. I stood and took two silent strides. I was standing seven or eight inches from him and in a single, fluid movement I delivered a right hook to his kidneys that would have floored a rhinoceros. He grunted and sagged, and made a weird, "Oooh..." sound, like he was sad.

I knew I was in trouble, and he hadn't dropped his weapon. I stepped to my right and forward, grabbed his right wrist, and twisted savagely away from me, like I was slowing a motorbike. He didn't let go of the pistol, so I kicked him in the balls and then I kicked him again in the knee. Finally I smashed the heel of my left hand into his elbow, grabbed the barrel of the weapon and wrenched it from his hand.

My reward for all my efforts was a left hook that caught me on the forehead and sent me crashing across the landing. I heard the gun clatter somewhere, but I had no idea where. I reached in my pocket for the Smith and Wesson, but a hand like a small moon grabbed hold of my collar and dragged me to my feet. For a second my vision was filled with a face as huge as it was ugly. I remember thinking, *It's not human*, before he drove his fist into my floating ribs, driving all the air out of my lungs.

I made a noise like furniture being dragged across a tiled floor as I tried to suck in air, and he threw me against the banisters. I managed not to fall over them, fell to the floor instead and made some more ugly noises. He towered over me and grunted, "*Kto ty?*"

I croaked, "What?"

He narrowed his already narrow eyes to slits beneath his huge brows. Frustration took over and he raised his booted foot to stamp down on my leg. I knew he would shatter my bone and some unconscious emergency protocol in my brain allowed the air to flow into my lungs. As he stamped down I bent both my knees and pulled back my legs, then smashed both my heels into his knees.

He bellowed like a wounded bull. I staggered to my feet, steadied myself and delivered two crashing hooks to his head. He groaned but he wouldn't go down, so I kicked him hard again in the same knee, clapped my open palms over his ears and, as he staggered back, drove my elbow into his chin.

He wavered for a moment and then crashed to the floor like a redwood tree.

I was still wheezing painfully. I had a screwdriver shoved through my temple and I was dizzy. I used his bootlaces to tie his ankles and went in search of the john. I found it, drank a gallon of water and splashed another gallon over my face and head. Then I filled a tooth mug and went back to see if this monster had morphed back into Bruce Banner yet. He hadn't. He still looked like an experiment human-stone hybridization that had gone horribly wrong. I splashed the water on his face. He blinked and grunted something in boulder language.

"*Kakaya?*"

I said, "Who are you?"

"*Kakaya?*"

"Who are you?"

He spat elaborately. "*Khuy tebe!*"

"Do you speak English?"

"You fuck English shit!"

I sighed. It was going to be pointless trying to interrogate this guy without an interpreter, and there was no way I could arrange that without admitting I had trespassed on his land and he had every right to try and shoot me. But if I let him go...

I pulled the wire cutters from my pocket and showed them to him. They were big and intimidating, the kind of thing favored by the Mafia's Internal Inquiries Department. He spat again.

I approached him, trod on his foot and applied the cutters to his Achilles tendon. I positioned it. I didn't squeeze. I just looked at him. He was scowling and started to make an inhuman noise, like a bear howling at the moon. His body started to tremble and my foot slipped off his. I looked at his legs. They had gone stiff, like two huge trembling tree trunks. Involuntarily I stepped back. He neck had swollen, his shoulder and his chest had swollen and the noise had become horrific.

Next thing his bootlaces had snapped and he was up on his feet, charging me. I acted without thinking, dropped and rolled, struggling to pull the revolver from my jacket. By the time I had got to my feet, all that was left of the banisters was a few broken matchsticks. He'd gone right through them. I ran down but the entrance was empty and the door was open and snow was drifting in. I ran out, but there was no sign of him save his footprints, which disappeared down the side of the building.

The wind was howling and freezing, and though the sun must have been rising beyond the clouds it was as dark as night still. I ran among the groaning, howling building. I could see from his prints that he was dragging one foot.

I came out to a broad patch of land that was probably a parking lot. There was a Land Rover there, with the door open and the lights on. The door slammed and the engine revved. I aimed and fired as the truck wheeled and hurtled away into the blackness behind the curtains of snow.

I turned and ran the way I had come, trying to get to the gate before him. I arrived at the courtyard just in time to see the truck ram the gate. He didn't quite make it, so he reversed and rammed again. I was still running but stopped, took careful aim and fired just as he accelerated and rammed a third time, ripping the gate off its hinges and bouncing over it out into the night.

I retraced my route, taking photographs with my cell phone of the dining room, the dorm, the wet footprints and finally the office. I grabbed as many files as I could carry and found the Hulk's semi-automatic. I was not surprised to see it was a GSh Tactical, with a Picatinny rail.

SEVEN

By the time I got back it was seven AM. It was still dark and the sky was still low and heavy. Four squares of warm light from her kitchen door provided the only color, and stained the snow in her backyard. I put the snowmobile back in her garage and when I came out I found her standing in the open door of her kitchen. She had a coffee pot and a kitchen towel in her hands. She spoke quietly:

"You OK?"

I closed the garage door and said, "I'm not sure. I might be dead and haven't realized it yet. I could use some of that coffee."

We went inside and I dumped my spoils on her large, pine table while she made coffee, waffles, bacon and eggs. Eventually she put it all on the table, sat opposite me and said, "You're bruised."

"There was somebody there. Must have been a caretaker."

She laid down her knife and fork. "Must have been? What is he now?"

"On his way to Canada."

"You going to tell me what happened any time soon?"

I pushed the files across the table to her, pulled over my plate and started to eat. I hadn't realized how hungry I was. I heard her leafing through the papers but focused on the eggs and the bacon, the waffles and the maple syrup. Eventually I drained my cup and sat back. She was staring at me.

"What the hell is this?"

"I learned a little Arabic and a little Spanish over the years. That's the extent of my linguistic skill, but I'd say that's Cyrillic script."

"Russian?"

"Probably, or Belarusian, Bulgarian, Serbian, Uzbek... There are quite a few Eastern European countries that use it."

She screwed up her brow. "You found these at the *mill?*"

I nodded. "Yeah, in a green metal filing cabinet of the sort the Army used to use in the '50s. It was in an office, locked."

"So what in the name of all that is holy, is a Canadian company logging in Maine doing storing files that are written in Russian?"

"I think that is the question." She went to speak several times but didn't, so I said, "The other question is, what do we do with this now?" I refilled my cup with hot, black coffee and said, "This has gone from being a hunt for a couple of killers to...what?"

She stared at me for a long moment. "You knew this, didn't you?"

I shook my head. "No. I had a hunch the logging company was not legit. But this is something else."

"What are you going to do?"

"I know what I am not going to do. I am not going to hand those over to the sheriff. The Feds need to see them."

She frowned. "How will you do that without admitting you broke in illegally?"

I smiled at her until she smiled and looked away. "I'll find a way," I said. "Meantime, I want to go over and see Doc Johansen before Sheriff Davies gets a hold of his findings."

She looked suddenly distressed. "You think they were raped, Harry?"

I shook my head again. "No, and that's what worries me."

"*What?*"

I stood and leaned on the table, looking down at her. "If they raped them, we know why they killed them. But if they didn't rape them, if the girls just showed up looking for help, why the hell did they kill them?"

Ten minutes later, in the car on the way to her restaurant, she said quietly, "Oh, my god..."

She dropped me at the morgue and I pushed inside out of the snow. It had started to ease, but it was still bitterly cold and the fall during the night had made drifts several feet deep.

I found Doc Johansen sitting at a small desk drinking black water from a paper cup. His eyes said he hadn't slept much. His mouth said, "What happened to you?"

"I told Helen I didn't like her waffles."

He smiled, then looked worried. "Seriously, that's a nasty bruise."

"You should see the other guy's fist. Did you look at the girls yet?"

"I was about to start."

I tried to make it sound casual and failed completely, "What have you arranged with the sheriff? You'll call him when you're done?"

He sighed heavily and sipped his brew. "If you must know, he told me to call him when I was done, and to let him know if you came prying."

"Is that what I am doing?"

He stood and studied me from under his eyebrows. "I don't know. Is it? What do you want, Mr. Bauer?"

He made his way across the room to where Suzy and Polly lay side by side, covered in white linen sheets. They had clearly thawed during the night. I let him fold back the sheet on Suzy and said, "I know for a fact they were murdered, Doc. There is no question of accidental death, or death by misadventure. They were murdered. The questions are how, and by whom?"

He had stopped, frozen, staring at the floor listening to me. I walked around to the other side of the autopsy table so I could look him in the face, and he could see mine.

"Doc, I aim to see that these girls' parents get justice. I hope you will help me do that. But if I have to put you and Sheriff Davies in prison to get the job done, make no mistake. I will do it." I leaned forward, with my hands on the table. "You want to know where I got this?" I pointed to the big bruise on my face. "I got it gathering evidence. And believe me, when the Feds see that evidence, and come asking questions, you do not want to be the author of a medical report that reads 'death by misadventure.'"

"Are you threatening me, Mr. Bauer?"

"Yup."

He combined a grunt with a sigh and set about organizing his instruments. Eventually he said, "I have no intention of falsifying the death certificate. I can't see any reason why I should."

"Maybe Sheriff Davies will provide you with a reason."

"I can't see any reason why he should, either."

"That's all dandy then, and we haven't got a problem. Mind if I sit in on the autopsy?"

"Be my guest," he said, like his mouth was full of lemon. "As long as you don't start throwing up."

I smiled pleasantly. "I don't see any reason why I should."

He glanced at me, then set about stripping Suzy's clothes from her body. After a couple of minutes, when she lay pale, blue-white naked on the steel table, he began to manipulate her head and her neck, recording what he was doing and what he was finding as he went.

He paused, looked at me and said, "Her vertebrae are broken."

I moved over and stood beside him, bent and peered closely at the bruises on her neck. I pointed at them and moved aside.

"Could whatever did that have broken her neck, Doctor Johansen?"

He gave me a look that said he knew I was also recording the session on my cell, then bent and spent a couple of minutes photographing and examining the bruises. When he was done I photographed them too.

"The bruises were caused by extreme pressure applied with the hands, and then by something long and hard."

"Like a forearm?"

"Yes, a powerful forearm might have caused it. There are no prints, so whoever did it was wearing gloves."

"So she was partially strangled, then whoever did this got her in a lock and broke her neck."

"And crushed her trachea, yes, that seems to be the most likely interpretation of the data so far. But," he nodded toward her abdomen and pointed, "I don't know if you've noticed. I saw them when I was removing her clothes. She has three very curious puncture wounds."

We bent over and examined them together. The were about an inch long and so fine, unless you were looking for them you could miss them.

"Notice," he said, "how there is slight damage to the skin at the bottom end of each incision—"

"But no bleeding."

"Exactly."

I went on, "I have seen this kind of wound before. It was made with a very sharp dagger, or a commando knife. The stabbing motion was up and under, which is why the lower part of the guard tore the skin. But..."

"Why no blood? She was already dead, but standing..."

"So one bastard held her and broke her neck, and the other stabbed her."

"I'm afraid that's what it looks like."

A cold rage twisted in my gut. "Were her clothes torn by the knife?"

He nodded. "She was dressed when she was stabbed. I am going to do the rape tests now."

I nodded. "Sure, do it. But I can tell you what you are going to find."

"You think they were raped?"

"I know they weren't. You don't rape your victim, dress them and then kill them. And you don't leave your victims, containing your DNA, a few yards from the roadside two miles from the nearest town, knowing there is going to be a search. It makes no sense."

He was frowning. "So if they were not killed to conceal the proof of rape, why were they killed?"

"To conceal something else."

He was very still, watching me. "Do you know what?"

"No, not yet."

There was a curious sucking sound and the door to the morgue moved and gave a small thud. For a moment the sound of the wind outside grew louder and was abruptly cut off. Then the door opened and the sheriff was standing there, frowning, looking from the doc to me like he was trying to catch our recent conversation by telepathy. After a moment he let the door swing closed behind him and took a few steps closer to the table. He stared at Suzy a moment, then raised his eyes to meet mine.

"Bauer, I thought I had made it clear to you—"

Suddenly I wasn't in the mood for his bullshit and I cut him dead. "The only thing you made clear to me, Davies, was that you are a piece of shit who isn't fit to wear that badge."

His face went crimson and his neck swelled. "Son of a bitch!"

"Can it, Jessie James. You are forty-eight hours away from a federal investigation. You want to keep your job and stay out of a federal penitentiary, you'd better clean up your act and get on the right side of the law." I pointed at the young, cold bodies. "These kids were murdered. They had their necks broken and Suzy was stabbed three times in the belly with a commando knife. You try to hush that up to keep your job and I'll have your badge and your job, and I'll make it so you can never show your miserable face in this town again."

He swallowed hard. "I don't know what you're talking about."

I stepped up close to him so I was looking down into his face, and growled, "Just do your damned job, you chicken-shit slob. You need to alert the state police, you need the sawmill to be raided and you need to put out a BOLO on a green Land Rover headed for the Canadian border. The driver has a broken leg and there may be several bullet holes in the chassis."

"Holy shit! What the hell have you done?"

"Exposed a skunk, by the looks of it."

"You're out of your mind!"

"Put out the BOLO, Sheriff."

"What have you *done?*" He stared at my face. "Those bruises," and again more quietly, "what have you done?"

I grabbed a fistful of his collar and dragged him toward me. "What have I done? Your damn job is what I've done! I walked into a rock and broke its leg, and it took off in a green Land Rover, but not before I put a few rounds into it. I also happened to stumble across a green steel filing cabinet that was full of files that are all written in Cyrillic script—that means Russian to you. So why don't you tell me, Sheriff? What *have* I done?"

He made three attempts at the T and finally stuttered, "Trespass..."

I shoved him away. "You don't get it, Walt. It's time to stop helping your Russian pals and start covering your own ass. Because as things stand, you're going down. Now, if I were you, I would get on the damned telephone to Machias and—"

"I can't!" His chest was rising and falling hard. "The telephone is down, cells have no coverage and the radio is not working. We're isolated till the storm eases."

I stabbed his chest with my finger. "Then you had better start putting together a posse, Walt! And as soon as the storm eases, you had better move into that sawmill and lock the whole damn place down."

"You'd better stop telling me what to do, Bauer. I'm getting pretty damn sick of it."

A hot rage welled up from my gut and with my left hand I

grabbed the back of his neck and dragged him across the floor to shove his face into Suzy's. He struggled to get free, but I roared at him, "*Look at her!*" Then I dragged him down till his face was an inch or two from her belly. "*Look at her, you son of a bitch!*"

"*Let go of me!*"

I dragged him up and spun him round and put him in a headlock, so my arm was around his neck and my mouth was by his ear.

"This is how he had her, you piece of shit! And while he crushed her windpipe and broke her neck, his pal was stabbing her in the gut. And you told her parents they got lost and died of cold, so you could hang on to your miserable job." I tensed the muscles in my arm and he began to choke. I rasped quietly in his ear, "Now you just do what I tell you, Walt, and be grateful I don't kill you right here. Are we on the same page now, Walt?"

I let go and shoved him. I knew he was dizzy through lack of air and he went down on his knees. He struggled to his feet. His face was crimson and he had tears streaming down his face. He searched for the doc with his eyes. "Doc, Doc, you saw what he did!"

The doc turned away and pulled back the sheet on Polly. The sheriff made a shrill noise in his throat. "*You saw what he did!*"

The doc ignored him. He turned to me. He was about to say something but I got there first.

"It only gets worse, Walt. Start organizing that posse. As soon as the snow stops, we want to move in." He swallowed and I went on. "Another thing, I am going to go to Machias to ask for help. I need a vehicle, and as soon as you can I need you to call ahead and let them know I am coming." He croaked something unintelligible. I patted him on the shoulder. "You're playing on our team now, Walt. Get used to it."

EIGHT

An hour later I left the morgue. The sky had turned a pale gray and looked close enough that you could reach up and touch it with your hand. It was still snowing, but it was more a case of desultory flakes drifting down like they weren't really sure where to go. The sheriff had left earlier, saying he was going to try and arrange a big truck with chains for me. He'd said to give him a couple of hours, but as I was passing in front of the sheriff's office Hank leaned out and called to me.

"Mr. Bauer? You got a moment?"

I approached across the sludge among the snowdrifts. "Sure, what up?"

"Sheriff would like to see you. He's in his office, in back. He said to go right on in."

I went behind the counter and crossed the wooden floor to the door that had "Sheriff" written on the glass panel in cold leaf. I knocked and opened the door without waiting for an answer. Sheriff Walt Davies was sitting behind his desk looking sore. I didn't sit down. I leaned on the back of the chair and looked at him. He raised both hands.

"Now don't go apeshit on me again. I am doing my best, and

as you have pointed out to me, it is in my interest to cooperate with you."

"But...?"

"But I cannot get you a vehicle before tomorrow morning."

"Bullshit. Why?"

"We have a snowplow. You want a snowplow?"

"Why not. It's perfect?"

"Because we sent it for servicing last week to the depot and the depot is two miles out of town on the Stony Lake Road. We have a RAM TRX with seven hundred horse power and six hundred and fifty foot pounds of torque. You want that baby?"

I nodded. "It should do the job."

"Yeah? Well it's at Hank's house with half the transmission on his garage floor. Which leaves the sheriff's Ford pickup, which is gonna get stuck in the snow and leave you stranded. Now if I thought you was gonna freeze to death overnight I might suggest you do it. But instead you're gonna force me to go and look for you. So goddammit, you'll have to wait till Hank has reassembled the Dodge!"

"Jesus Christ!" I shook my head. "What kind of a show are you running here, Walt? You have a snowstorm descending on you out of Canada and you tell your deputy to disassemble the transmission on one of the only snow-worthy vehicles you have, while the other is being serviced?"

"Obviously, when we took that decision..." He sagged and sighed, like he was giving up under the weight of all his poor choices. "You can have the RAM tomorrow morning. Take it or leave it."

"OK, meantime, keep trying to get through to them, and write me a letter or something, on your official paper. Don't go into detail, just tell them I'll fill them in."

"Yeah, yeah, fine. I'll do it. Now get the hell out of here, will you? You're giving me indigestion. Even my breakfast is turning against me."

I went to the door and put my hand on the handle, then paused, looking at him.

"What?"

"Maybe you should learn to chew properly."

"Get out of my office, Bauer."

I left, and with nothing much else to do, I made my way to Helen's restaurant. It was empty again, but for one customer. She was an elegant, elderly lady. I figured she was in her eighties, but in good shape. She had bright, humorous eyes that were slightly mocking, and a back that was as straight as a ramrod, whether she was sitting or standing. Helen was sitting with her, but stood as I came in and moved toward me.

"Harry, this is Miss Rosie Harrison. We were just discussing everything that's been going on," she widened her eyes at me meaningfully, then smiled and asked, "You want a coffee?"

"Coffee would be nice." I went over to the table and held out my hand. "How do you do, Miss Harrison?"

She laid her hand in mine with a hint of mischief in her eyes and spoke in a voice that had been there and done that, and kept the wet T-shirt. "I do just fine, Harry, and call me Rosie, will you? You'll only make me feel old if you call me miss."

"All right, Rosie. Mind if I join you?"

"I was hoping you would. Now, you mustn't be cross with Helen, Harry."

"Why would I be?"

"You must be cross with me, because I am very good at wheedling things out of people."

"Wheedling. It sounds like it requires skill."

"As if, it sounds *as if* it requires skill. Like is adjectival, it goes with a noun. As if is adverbial and goes with a verb or a phrase. Never mind. It does require skill, and it's a skill I have, and I have made poor Helen tell me things she didn't want to tell me."

I smiled. "About what?"

"You see, I may look to you like a simple old lady—"

"Not at all. You look to me like a very complicated young lady."

She liked that. She threw her head back and hooted with laughter. "Oh!" she said, "you are a *very* bad boy!"

"And you are a very naughty lady. So why don't you tell me what this is about?"

I said it with a smile and she met my eye with a smile of her own. She had tested me and not found me wanting. She and Helen exchanged some kind of signal and Helen came over with a pot of coffee and a cup for me.

"I used to be a professor at Harvard, you know."

I made an appropriately impressed face and asked, "What was your field?"

"Anthropology. I had a very promising career. I loved my subject, which I combined with social psychology. I was writing a book."

I sipped my coffee. "You make it sound like—" I stopped and smiled. "You make it sound *as if* something happened to wreck your plans."

She smiled at Helen, like she was in the know. "Oh, yes. Something happened. Isaac happened." I waited. Her gaze went first to the counter and then out to the snow, but you knew she was seeing neither. She was seeing a procession of images and movies inside her own head.

"My family settled here before the War of Independence. My great, great, great...," she waved her hand in the air, "great-grandfather came here with his wife in the seventeenth century. James Harrison. He was a staunch Anglican, as they were called then. He built a house which I still own for himself and his wife and his five children. That was almost four hundred years ago. We have produced doctors, lawyers, vicars, and in my generation a professor of anthropology who was going to publish a standard work on social psychology and anthropology."

There was a challenge in her eye when she looked at me, like it was somehow my fault, along with the rest of the world, that it hadn't worked out. I arched an eyebrow.

"And then Isaac came along?"

She looked away. "That was over fifty years ago, half a century. It was my great, great-grandfather who built the vicarage. The town was more up that way in those days. He was an obstinate man, an admirer of Wesley, you understand, but adhered to Anglicanism saying there was no need for the church to split." She sighed. "But of course in the end we all became Methodists."

I smiled. "I'm a little lost."

She blinked at me a few times. "Aren't we all? The thing is, we had always considered the Boothes to be upstarts because they only showed up in the 1800s. I mean, I think they had only been here ten or fifteen years when the Civil War broke out. They came from Lancashire, in England, and added an 'e' to their name to seem more distinguished. But they were just farmers. Common farmers."

"The Boothes," I said, hoping it would prompt her into explaining what the hell she was talking about.

"Exactly."

"Isaac was a Boothe?"

"Of course."

"They settled in Balthazar in the mid 1800s—"

"Isn't that what I said?"

"No, you implied it."

"I mean, we practically *founded* this village. Balthazar was my great, great, great many times uncle."

"And I am deducing that Isaac was also at Harvard?"

"Of course." She smiled at Helen. "You're quite right. He is not stupid." To me she said, "Where did you go to university, Harry?"

I didn't smile. I said, "The village of Al-Landy, Helmand Province, Afghanistan."

She nodded. "I understand."

"That's where I got my PhD in human behavioral studies. So what was Isaac Boothe with an 'e' doing at Harvard?"

"Being a genius. He was utterly brilliant. He shone. His field was psychiatry. He had his medical degree, he had *devoured* his specialization psychology and neurology, he was in analysis so that he could qualify as a Freudian psychoanalyst, and while he was at it, so as not to become bored, he kept up to speed in architecture, astronomy, physics—quantum *and* relativity, mathematics..."

"He was smart and you fell in love with him."

"Don't be impertinent." And then, "Of course I did."

"You fell in love with a Boothe with an 'e.' Was that the problem?" I glanced at Helen with a face that asked what the hell I was doing talking to this character. She looked at me with eyes that said I shouldn't jump to conclusions and I should stay with it. Miss Rosie Harrison said, "No, that was part of the attraction."

"This was the sixties, you were a rebel."

She smiled. "Exactly," she sighed, "and so was he."

"Ah, this would be shortly after the Timothy Leary scandal, when Leary and Ginsberg were leading the counterculture."

"You got it. Isaac just loved it. He was handsome, young enough at thirty-five to be attractive to his students, but old enough to be a figure of authority. He experimented with just about everything there was to experiment with. I think he once even mainlined gin. He said the hangover almost drove him to suicide. He did orgies, field trips to Mexico to experiment with peyote, and I just found him utterly irresistible."

"What happened?"

"Oh." She sighed heavily and shook her head. "He was writing some trash, a book, which was a deeply unoriginal blend of Freudian case studies and Carlos Castaneda. It was self-indulgent, facile, undisciplined trash. If he had published it as a Harvard professor he would have sold millions and he would have been up there with Leary, Ginsberg and the Beatles. But that didn't happen."

Now that she had stopped playing the cute pussycat, I was

becoming interested. I couldn't see yet how this tied up with Suzy and Polly, but I could smell the connection was there.

"What did happen?"

"They fired him. But they had learned their lesson from Timothy Leary, and this time they covered their asses and they made him sign an agreement."

"What kind of agreement?"

"They would pay him a generous pension and he would agree not to publish his book, or any other book that purported to be based on his experiences at Harvard. He would also agree not to engage in any activities that might bring Harvard's name into disrepute. Of course the beauty of it for them was that if they withdrew his pension for any reason, it would be up to *him* to sue *them*, at his expense and going up against the most eminent legal minds in the country."

"And he agreed."

"Oh, yes. He agreed. The pension was generous. It was in line with a senior Harvard professor's salary and linked to inflation. It offered him a very comfortable living without ever having to work again in his life. Just so long as he didn't cause any public scandals."

There was a moment's silence. Outside somebody trudged by dressed like an Eskimo, with the snow up to mid-shin. I said, "But when the shit hit the fan it sprayed, right?"

She nodded. "It sprayed and it stuck. Half his class were kicked out for behavior liable to bring the university into disrepute, and I was kicked out for having been a close associate of his, for attending his parties and for engaging in experiments with illegal hallucinogens. But of course, I was not a high-profile genius. So there was no pension for me, not even a payoff, just, 'Get your things, clear your office and haul ass!'"

"Rough justice."

"Just rough. No justice at all."

I glanced at Helen. Rosie caught the look and smiled.

"When you get to my age, Harry, I figure you have earned the right to ramble and make people listen to you. I know you're looking for the men who killed Suzy and poor Polly. So let me tell you straight away that I do not know who did that terrible thing, or why. And it may be that what I am going to tell you has absolutely *nothing* to do with their deaths."

"OK, I understand. What is it you want to tell me?"

"When Isaac was kicked out of Harvard, two things happened to him. One, he got bored. And like the Marquis de Sade, the one thing he could not tolerate, above all others, was boredom. The other thing that happened was that he found a professor's salary, even a senior professor's salary, was nowhere near enough to assuage his boredom when he had nothing to do all day but spend his money. So he sought to set up a business that would make him rich, an at the same time, relieve his boredom."

"Oh," I said and nodded. "Now I begin to see the connection. What, exactly, was this business?"

"If you are thinking drug trafficking or anything like that, you are way off base. He set up a movie studio in his house. He has a big house just outside town which he inherited from his parents, and he converted part of it to a movie studio."

I arched an eyebrow. "A movie studio... What kind of movie studio?"

"That kind of movie studio. He sails right on the edge of legality, exactly where he most likes to be. He claims his movies are not pornographic, but erotic and a legitimate artistic expression protected by the Constitution. But for every tastefully erotic movie he makes, he makes five which would make your hair turn gray."

"Forgive me, Rosie," I smiled, showing my apology was sincere and not ironic, "how do you know this? Is this hearsay, or do you know for a fact that he makes hardcore pornography?"

"I know it for a fact. We have stayed in touch over the years. I was once his girlfriend, you know, until we were kicked out. I blamed him and resented that I didn't get paid off, as he did. So we didn't speak for a while. But he was always a charmer and eventually he invited me over to see his studio. His name doesn't appear in the credits, to keep Harvard happy, but he is the producer. And he showed me some of the more unsavory examples of his work. Quite disgusting."

"How long has he been making them?"

"Years. I believe he started in the nineties, after traveling the world, writing unsuccessful novels, doing all sorts of stuff, he set up his studio. I believe it is quite successful."

I rubbed my face, feeling suddenly very tired, wondering how this new item fit into the overall picture—or indeed if it did at all.

"Let me ask you, Rosie, what connection do you, personally, think the studio has with Suzy's and Polly's death?"

She hesitated, then she hesitated some more. "I'm not sure. I wouldn't like to speculate. But I can tell you that two things Isaac loves are flaunting the law, and seeking thrills."

"How old is Isaac now, Rosie?"

"Oh, in his early eighties, I'd say. That is in years. But in his mind and spirit? He is somewhere between four and nineteen! A very dangerous age indeed!"

NINE

SHE GOT TO HER FEET AND PLACED A HAND ON MY shoulder.

"Don't get up. It was good talking to you. This has troubled me for many years," she spoke to Helen, with her hand still on my shoulder. "Nothing ever came of it, so I suppose I came to accept it. But now this..." She patted my shoulder. "Thank heavens the Lord has sent us this young warrior. Only God knows what we would do if it was left in Walt's hands."

She patted my shoulder once more and made her way, very stiff and erect, toward the door. When she was almost there I stood and said, "Rosie?" She stopped and turned. I said, "Why are the ages between four and nineteen dangerous?"

She stared at me a long time, like she was surprised by the question but didn't want to show it. Finally she said:

"Because the person is still largely driven by the uncontrolled impulses of the id, greed, the uncompromising need for instant gratification, organic impulses which are not tempered by the ego or the superego. Once we reach our late teens and adulthood, the id is brought to heel," she smiled, "most of the time." She hesitated, became abstracted and looked out at the cold, gray street. "But in some cases the id remains dominant, the person never develops a superego, the ego is left weak and unable to control those primal urges. The person has no respect for society, for social mores and customs, or for other people for that matter. And these people can become dangerous, Harry, because other people's lives end up having little or no value for them."

I nodded briefly. "Rosie, do you know of any connection Isaac may have with Russia, or the Russian mob?"

She looked nonplussed. "Not that I know of, no." Then she gave a laugh that was all about exhaustion. "But with Isaac you never know. Even in his eighties he is impossible to keep up with."

She reached for the door but I stopped her.

"Who does he sell his movies to?"

Again the smile. "All sorts of people all over the world, mostly websites I think. But he works through a distributor, so that Harvard are neither alerted not upset. And before you ask me, I believe it is some man across the border in Canada. I have not been close to Isaac for many, many years, Harry. Occasionally he contacts me to try and upset me, but that is about the size of it."

"Thank you."

She waited a moment. He smile deepened. "May I go now?"

"Of course, I'm sorry to have kept you."

She opened the door, allowing in the cold and the wind for a moment, and left. She walked stiffly across the snow to a large, dark blue Range Rover with chains on its wheels. A big black guy in a suit jumped out, opened the door for her and helped her in.

A moment later they were gone and I stood looking at the melted snow where they had been seconds earlier. I turned to Helen who was still sitting, staring at the coffee pot.

"What was that all about?"

She looked up at me and said simply, "Isaac Boothe. A notorious son of Balthazar that most people prefer not to talk about."

"Where does he live?"

"He has a lakeside house in its own grounds about a quarter of a mile from my place."

"Will you take me to see him?"

She looked around at her empty restaurant and shrugged. "Not much else to do. But I don't know if he'll see us, Harry. He's been a recluse for years. When the scandal broke the town was not supportive, as you can imagine. He went and locked himself in his house and has barely been heard from since."

"He'll see me."

She frowned. "What makes you so sure?"

"I'm from New York, and I am fascinated by him. To a narcissist like him, that will be irresistible."

She made a face, shrugged and set about cleaning up. Ten minutes later we were on our way back to her place, doing ten miles an hour trying not to slip and slide on the sludge. At her house we dropped the car in the garage and took the snowmobile. The heavy snow that had fallen during the night and the early morning was easing, but the gunmetal sky was still bellying low and oppressive, and the flakes were still falling; slow and wispy, but without let.

Isaac Boothe with an "e" was short, about five four. He had a round, bald head like an overinflated balloon spread with Vaseline, his two front teeth were missing and he had round, insolent eyes that were there to tell you they really didn't give a damn; and if you asked him what about they'd ask you back, "Whatcha got?"

He had wrenched open the door and now stood looking us over up and down.

"Who are you?" Then he pointed to me and said, "You," and turning to Helen he added, "I know who you are. You're from the restaurant." His expression of insolence slipped into a leer. "I watch you pour coffee sometimes. I like the way you pour coffee, little joke, a cock of the hip. Why don't you do that for me sometime?"

"Mr. Boothe?" I said.

"What? I asked you who you were."

"My name is Harry Bauer—"

"That's your name!" he snapped. "People don't understand anymore. We knew, you see, we knew it wasn't the same. We'd say,

'Hey man, who am I? Who are you? Like what does it *mean?* The question is, *what is the question?* Right?'"

I made no effort to conceal the sigh. "OK, Mr. Boothe," and then narrated in a monotone, "Hey man, who am I? Who are you? Like what does it mean? The question is, what is the question? Right? Now, are we done?" Before he could put his expression of disgust into words, I pushed on. "I would like to talk to you and ask you some questions. I know about your time at Harvard, and I know you have some pretty controversial views on morality and sex..."

I trailed off. I knew I had done enough. His narcissism had taken over and he didn't give a damn who I was or why I was there. He was going to spend the next hour telling me all about his time at Harvard and his controversial views on morality and sex.

"You CIA or something? I'm not afraid of you." He turned and walked inside, talking as he went in a loud, strident voice. "You want to come in? Come on in! What do you want, gin and tonic? Vodka? A joint? You want a joint? Or we can snort some lines of coke if you want. Name it?"

I followed him in and Helen came behind me. I said, "Not this time. Maybe next time."

We were in a large entrance area of highly polished, dark wooden floorboards. There was a coat stand with a mirror and a small table, a small settee and then a couple of steps down to a very ample living room and dining room. The furniture was modern but not minimalist. Nothing about Isaac Boothe could ever be minimalist. The sofa was calico, vast and overstuffed, slanted at a crazy angle in front of an open fireplace that would have looked at home in a Tudor manor, and where logs the size of rafters were already burning. There were books floor to ceiling on bookcases, and also stacked in piles on the floor, and the chairs were placed more for easy access to the books than to create a space for sitting and talking, or enjoying the fire. Everything was chaotic, though it seemed to obey a private logic of its own.

Isaac fell on the sofa and slung his arm over his eyes.

"What do you want?" he said.

Helen sat in the chair nearest the fire, and I dragged the other overstuffed calico monster across the floor so I was close to the sofa. Then I sat. He raised his arm and gazed at me a moment. "Make yourself at home, won't you?"

"I plan to. Why'd they kick you out of Harvard?"

He groaned, like people asked him that every day and he was tired of answering it. My guess was nobody had asked him in forty years and he would have paid good money to be able to tell somebody again.

"Let me ask you something, Harry Bauer." He said it with his arm still laid across his eyes. "Have you ever been to a university?" He uncovered his eyes to look at me. "I mean a *good* university?"

"No. Tell me about it."

"These temples, these great halls of learning..." he sat up, like Duncan rising from the dead to denounce Macbeth, "these monuments to the human intellect, are halls of *lies!* They are monuments, oh yes..." He sat nodding, with his arms hanging between his knees and his fingers trailing on the carpet. "Oh yes, they are monuments—to the towering egos of the professors who make up the board of trustees. Each building, each edifice, each faculty is a totem to the phallus, to the *cock and balls*, of the president, the provost, and the deans of the university! These monuments have nothing to do with learning, or truth. They are all about the vast, phallic egos of those monstrous posers. None of these monuments are to the woman's *kólps*, because the women who rise to those heights all fantasize that they have huge, male phalli!"

He spread his legs and held out his hands like he was holding a huge beach ball, screwed up his face and emitted a shrill cackle.

I shrugged. "What has this to do with you getting kicked out?"

He gaped, spread his hands, shook his head. "Well, only *everything!*"

I looked at Helen and sighed like I was getting bored. "This is a waste of time."

He didn't give her time to answer.

"Oh, I am boring you? The man who almost turned the Western establishment on its head, the man whom Tim Leary called his heir apparent, the man who almost resurrected the counterculture, only he was crushed, beaten and muzzled by the establishment, is *boring you?*" He pointed at me and I saw his pale, soft cheeks flush red. "Well let me give you some advice, Harry Bauer: you should open your ears, and open your heart and maybe, just maybe, your soul might benefit from my words. Because I have been to places you have never been, I have probed shadows you have not dared to sniff, and I have eaten the soft underbelly of the human soul."

I shrugged. "Yeah, maybe you have, but all you do is talk about talking about it. But you never actually talk about it. You keep telling me how amazing you are, but you never tell me what you did that was so damned amazing. You know what I think? I think your Harvard deans, who put in sixteen hours a day putting together empirical evidence for their papers, are the real thing. And I think you are full of hot air and shit, and all you know how to do is blow your own mind."

"Oh," he laughed, "I could blow yours, pal!"

"How, by feeding me lysergic acid? Anyone can do that, Isaac. You don't need an IQ of a hundred and fifty, or to be a new age prophet to do that. Any asshole can do that. I came here looking for real wisdom, experience, *life*. And all I find is a spoilt kid griping about the one that got away."

For a moment I wondered if I'd gone too far. He was angry, but more than that I had bruised his vanity, and I was guessing this was the first time he had had anyone actually wanting to listen to him for a very long time.

"OK, wiseass." He picked up a bamboo box from a lamp table beside the sofa and fingered out a cigarette. Just below the brown tip I could make out the word Camel in blue letters. He gave

Helen a sneering smile. "Do you mind if I smoke? I don't mind if you mind."

He lit up with a pink, disposable lighter and dragged the smoke deep into his lungs where he held it for a long moment before exhaling. He grinned at me. "Dead giveaway."

I said, "Does this ever end?" He flicked ash. "All this noise and bullshit and clowning, does it ever stop? Because I heard there was this amazing guy. Everything you said: the man who almost turned the Western establishment upside down, the man whom Timothy Leary called his heir apparent, the man who almost resurrected the counterculture, the man who has been to places I have never been, who has probed the shadows and *eaten* the soft underbelly of the human soul, the man who scared Harvard into sacking him and paying him for his silence." I gestured at him. "But all I see is a guy who talks about how he *could* talk about things, but he never does. All he does is clown about, talk bullshit and try to shock people who are past shocking by saying 'vagina' in Greek."

I sighed like I was disappointed, put my hands on my knees and stood. He said: "Wait."

I waited.

He sucked on his cigarette and let out the smoke through his nose and his mouth as he spoke.

"There is a temple in Nepal which, on the outside, is covered in the most extraordinary golden statues and carvings. But, when you go inside, the temple is empty, devoid of any decoration, and if you should ask the monks why that is, they will tell you that it is quite deliberate. Those who come seeking to be awed and amazed by extraordinary things will stay on the outside. Those seeking learning and wisdom, will come inside. I guess I do something similar. I put on the show and most people, especially the chicks, cuddle up to the clown, snort the coke and smoke the marijuana. Very few tell me to cut the crap and get real."

He took another drag on his cigarette, held the smoke down and let it out in a long stream.

"But I can get real," he said. "I can get very real."

"Yeah? How real?"

"Life and death real. Is that real enough for you?"

"I don't know what that means. It's more words, Isaac."

He shook his head. "No. Have you ever looked into the eyes of death, Harry Bauer? Have you ever seen a human soul cease to exist? It's like looking into a light bulb, and flipping off the switch. Have you ever done that?"

"Have you?"

He nodded. "Oh, yeah. I told you, I can get very real."

TEN

"You make porn movies?"

"I make *erotic* movies."

"You want to explain the difference?"

Helen was still sitting, watching Isaac with no expression on her face. Isaac flapped back on his overstuffed sofa and rolled his eyes to the ceiling.

"Well the first is how sad and grubby the mind of the viewer is. When *you* see the naked human form, what do you do? Do you see a thing of beauty, or do you..."

"OK, I get it. One is the subjective appreciation of the viewer. What's the other?"

"Oh my goodness, the ape can think! The other is simply this: in erotic art, the piece of art—the painting, the photograph, the story, the movie—is all about the subject. The woman, the couple, whatever; your attention as the viewer is focused on *them.* In pornography it's all about you. The subject is a lump of meat, and your attention as the viewer is focused on your feelings of arousal."

"And you make erotic movies rather than pornography."

"Uh-huh, that's what I said."

"Where is your market?"

He screwed up his face and his jaw went slack. "What?"

"Your market. Who do you sell this erotic art to?"

His eyes shifted, first to the big logs burning in the fire, then to the dining area over on the far side of the room. "I dunno," he said at last. "I have an agent. He buys them from me and sells them or distributes them or whatever they do."

"You expect me to believe that?"

He screwed up his face again. This time the expression was not confusion. It was pugnacious. His lip curled so I could see the gap in his teeth.

"Not really. See, I don't give a shit what you believe. You came here asking questions, and I don't need to tell you a damned thing. Fuck you. Tell me, am I too ambiguous for you?"

"Who's your agent?"

"Fuck you."

I crossed the room and stood looking out through his sliding glass doors at the snow. It wasn't so much a blanket as a vast pile of Nordic duvets.

"Your motivation," I said, still staring out at the white world broken here and there by the stenciled black fingers of dead trees, "is the search for truth."

There was silence. I turned and saw him craning over the back of the sofa to look at me. He slung his left arm over to make it easier and said, "OK."

"What is truth to you?"

He threw back his head and laughed out loud, barking his laughter at the ceiling. Finally he shook his head, grinning at me. "I am that I am. Can truth ever be subjective? Does the subjective not become objective when it is truth?"

I walked over to him and bent down to look into his eyes. I saw he was excited by the attention.

"Life and death real, Isaac. Have you ever looked into the eyes of death? Have you ever seen a human soul cease to exist, like looking into a light bulb, and flipping off the switch? Have you ever done that?"

"Yeah."

I smiled. "Recently?"

"No."

"When, Isaac?"

He turned and looked at Helen, like she had asked him the question.

"Years ago, in Mexico. One of the trips we made to do mescaline." He glanced at me, then back at Helen. "It's not only present in peyote buds, you know? You get it from the Peruvian torch, the San Pedro..."

I sighed. "You going to go rambling off again, Isaac?"

He rubbed his round, shiny face.

"There was a dog. A real sweet, friendly dog. We were in a village, Topahue, twenty, thirty miles east of Hermosillo. It was like—*remote*—man. And if you were like this *famoso Americano doctore*, you could just do *anything*, amigo! We had more peyote than you could ever consume, we had marijuana, we had tequila, we had *señoritas*, we had a *ball*. Man, I didn't come down to Earth in all the time I was there. We just tripped and made love and got high..." He leered at Helen. "You would have loved it, baby. You know what free means, kiddo?"

"Isaac?"

He sighed. "So, it's a trippy place, when you spend two weeks disconnected from the chains of this shit version of reality."

"So you killed a dog."

Now he turned to look at me. "You have to make it sound like that?"

"How should it sound, Isaac. You tell me?"

"He was sick of being a dog, man! I looked into his big, moist brown eyes and I could hear his soul crying out to me. He wanted to be free! He wanted to come back as a man! He was there, in our commune, digging us all exploring our consciousness, being free, expanding our souls, and this poor little guy was trapped in the body of a *chucho* in fuckin' Mexico, man." He scratched his upper lip and smiled. "So I spent a whole day sharpening a kitchen knife till it was so sharp you could hold a hair between your fingers and just *whoosh*! Slice it in half."

I walked back to my chair and sat. He had his mouth gaping in a smile, watching me.

"So in the evening, as the sun was going down, we made a fire, and I called *Chucho* over to me and we lay together on a Mexican blanket. And I held his face, looking into his big, brown eyes, and everybody was watching us, sending kind of love and good vibes for *Chucho*. And I just gently, lovingly, slipped that sharp knife into his heart. He struggled and kicked for a moment, but I watched his dog life die in his eyes. And then he was at peace, so he could come back as a free spirit. It was real."

"You ever kill a person?"

He gave a soft laugh. "If I had, I wouldn't tell you about it. I know you." He stabbed his finger at me. "You can come here in disguise, but I know you. We had a name for you back then. You are The Man. You are the Man of Violence. You hit people and kick people and you kill people, to make sure we all conform, man. The history of Man is the history of the free spirit against the Hive. And you are the soldier ant, keeping everyone in line. You know? Zeppelin?" He sang embarrassingly out of tune, "And said hey please would we all, get in line! Get in line!"

"You heard about Suzy and Polly?"

He produced his gaping grin again. "What did Suzy and Polly do? Were Mommy and Daddy very cross?"

"They were murdered."

The smile faded from his face. Now he looked distasteful. "I know. I heard. I figured it would be just a matter of time before they started pointing the finger at the disgusting old pervert by the lake."

"Tell me about your Canadian agent."

"Larry?"

"Are you asking me or telling me?"

"His name is Larry Gaynor. He lives in Quebec, the city. Why?"

"Does he buy and sell lumber, too?"

Again the screwed-up face. "*What?*"

Helen spoke suddenly, "Does he own the sawmill, Isaac?"

He shrugged and shook his head like we'd asked him if he had webbed toes. "No...? I don't know? Maybe he does? I have no idea."

I said, "How'd you meet him?"

"He was a student before they kicked me out for being free. He approached me a few years after I'd left and proposed the movie thing."

"Where's the studio?"

"Right here in my house. You want to see it?"

I nodded. "Yeah."

He jumped up from the sofa and crossed the dining room to a black spiral metal staircase that rose through the ceiling to the upper floor. We followed him up and came to a broad landing with blond wooden floors. There was a blue sofa, a coffee table with magazines and a long corridor straight ahead.

Isaac marched down that passage, throwing open the doors as he passed them. He didn't so much speak over his shoulder, as announce what he was saying to the world at large, to all those who would listen, and those who wouldn't, too.

"Studio one, the bedroom, studio two, the living room and the bearskin rug in front of the fire, studio three, the dining room, studio four, the biggest, where we can construct any set we like." He stopped and pushed open a fifth door at the end. "The storeroom, cameras, lights, blah blah blah."

I looked into the bedroom. The windows were closed, as were the drapes. I switched on the light and saw a big, brass bed, a couple of bedside tables, little else. The living room showed a large sofa, a couple of armchairs and, as he had said, a large bearskin rug in front of a fireplace. As we moved from one to the next he waited for us at the end, by the storeroom.

"I have a converted stable out back with lots more furniture, so we can do period pieces, Westerns, exotic, science fiction... You name it."

I looked in at the large, bare room at the end. "You write, direct and perform?"

He laughed out loud. "Not any more. I just provide the studio and some of the money. I have kind of lost interest."

"What happens if you get blown?"

He looked genuinely surprised. "Blown? I told you, there is nothing illegal about this. The worst that could happen is that there is a lot of publicity and Harvard withdraws my pension. But the fact is I make a lot more money from the movies than I do from Harvard. It would be unfortunate, but hardly a catastrophe."

We were standing close, cramped in the corridor. I looked him in the eye. "You alone here?"

He nodded.

"Did you kill Suzy and Poppy?"

His face flushed red. "Good God! I mean, why? Because I took drugs and make dirty pictures? No! For God's sake!"

"Do you know who did?"

"Look...*no! OK?* Christ! I mean, do *not* be different, kids!" His voice became shrill. "Whatever you do in this life, *do not be different! They will hunt you down and kick you to the ground and stamp on you until they eradicate you completely!*"

Helen turned abruptly and walked away. After a moment I followed her down the stairs, with Isaac some way behind us. He eventually caught up with us at the front door. His shrill hysteria was gone, replaced by a mocking smile.

"Going so soon? Won't you stay for dinner and sex? I am pretty good at both, as it happens."

"Thanks for your time."

"Curt, dismissive, superior. I don't know who you are, Harry Bauer, but my only crime in this world has been not toeing the line. My crime has been seeking my own path, seeking freedom."

I nodded. "That, and killing a defenseless dog that trusted

you, just so you could find out what it felt like." I stepped up close to him. "Did you try it with Suzy and Polly, too? To see what it felt like to kill two defenseless girls? You want to try it on me, Isaac, and see what it feels like to kill a mean son of a bitch?"

I opened the door and stepped out into the ice-cold whiteness of the day. It felt good. He watched us from the doorway as we climbed onto the snowmobile and turned, to drive out the gate and back onto the road: the winding stretch of sludge lying between two high banks of thick, white snow.

The whine of the engine was loud under the pines as we sped through the woods. I called back to her, "Your place or the restaurant?"

"Collect the car, then the restaurant!" she shouted above the freezing wind. "I need to work!"

I smiled, wondering if she'd have any clients other than me, and headed for her house.

We swapped the snowmobile for the car and rolled up at the restaurant twenty minutes later. The place was a desolate snowscape. The whole town seemed to have been deserted, and what had been an ice-cold breeze earlier, as the day progressed was turning into an icy wind that would slice through your flesh like a frozen blade. We clambered out of the vehicle, slammed the doors and ran, huddled, for the warmth of the restaurant. There we bundled inside and slammed the door, shutting out the bluster and the swirling flakes of snow.

Helen hurried to the kitchen to make hot coffee while I stamped my feet and clapped my hands. Eventually I peeled off my gloves and my jacket and she came out to lean on the counter.

"So what you're thinking," she said, "is that this Canadian guy—"

"Larry Gaynor—"

"Yeah, Larry Gaynor, is involved with the Russian Mafia in the porn industry. Part of their operation is at Isaac's house,"

"We saw the studio," I said.

"Which," she snapped her fingers, "OK, OK, how's this. The

operation is divided between his house and the sawmill. Russian Mafia own the sawmill and the Canadian guy and Isaac provides the movie equipment et cetera. Now, Isaac runs a legitimate *erotic* studio at his house, in case anyone should ever inquire, but at the sawmill they are running a much more pornographic operation which is also much more lucrative. But Isaac has complete deniability."

I nodded. "Seems likely something like that is going on."

"So when Suzy and Polly went to get help, they walked in on, God alone knows what. Studio equipment being hauled in or out, a bunch of actors and actresses, something that gave away what was *really* going on at the mill. So they had to be silenced. Because not only would Isaac lose his Harvard pension—which must be a lot more than he made it out to be—but an investigation into his connection with the sawmill would also show that he was not into artistic erotica, but triple-X porn, with maybe a sideline of drugs thrown in for good measure. I don't see Isaac as a guy who goes for half-measures."

I grunted and nodded. "It has to be something very like that." I scratched my head. "So are we saying he was there? Did he see it happen? Or did they just stumble on a couple of Russians..." I trailed off, not sure really what I was asking. "We need some physical evidence, or some witness testimony, to connect Isaac with the sawmill. Right now all we have is the fact that he is a particularly unpleasant person. But we didn't see or hear anything that said he was involved in criminal activity." I studied her face for a minute, where she stood behind the counter. "A narcissist, an ego freak, perhaps even a genuine seeker after truth. Not someone you would want your daughter to date. But bottom line there was nothing in what he said or did or possessed in his house, to connect him to Suzy and Polly."

"You know what you need, don't you?"

"A hot soup, a burger and a beer?"

"You need a confession. Now, a Wyoming man would know just how to git one a' them, cowboy style."

"Well, I think I'd know how to git one o' them too, farmgirl, but I'm hoping I can hand this over to the state police tomorrow, and let them finish the job."

She sighed. "I hope you're right."

"Me too."

But we both knew we had a bad feeling, and we both knew why.

ELEVEN

I was in need of an early night and a good sleep, so I made my way back to my house on Water Street, where I had barely set foot since I arrived, after an early dinner at Helen's Family Restaurant. She had wanted to drive me, but it was just a half-mile walk, and it was probably safer walking than driving anyway. And besides, I needed the cold air to clear my head and cool me down.

The streets were empty. The occasional passage of cars and the efforts of the mayor's office to clear the roads had left rivers of gray sludge between sidewalks piled high with drifts of snow, tinged yellow by the streetlamps.

I passed the Naughty Little Seafood Shack, the gray clapboard Laundromat with the white-trimmed colonial porch, and came finally to my rental house. It looked suddenly cold and uninviting and for a moment I toyed with the idea of going back and spending the night with Helen. Instead I shoved the key in the lock, let myself in and flipped on the light.

The door gave straight onto the living room. It was broad and spacious, with wooden floors, several heavy rugs and an open fireplace with a big, stone chimneybreast. It should have been cozy and welcoming. Instead it was bleak and vaguely depressing.

I crossed to the mantelshelf over the fireplace, to where I had the bottle of Bushmills I had brought with me, popped the cork and poured myself a generous measure. A sudden sense of unease made me turn. The room was empty, still and very quiet. The dim light from the two overhead bulbs reflected on the polished table. Beyond it the glass in the sliding doors was black. I went and closed the drapes. Then I stood listening. The silence was so complete it became almost white noise in my ears.

The kitchen had the same empty stillness. I pulled the blue, gingham curtains across the black glass and climbed the stairs to the bedrooms. There were three of them and each was empty, still and silent. I pulled the drapes across the dark glass and the rattle of the wooden rings on the rails sounded loud through the house. And my feet thumped on the stairs as I went back down to get my whiskey from the dining table.

For a moment I wondered about Isaac. I wondered what, if anything, lay beneath the crazy act. How did a guy like that get admitted to Harvard as a professor in the '60s? Maybe he got progressively more crazy as the years went by and he burned out his reserves of neurons.

I found my glass and sipped, standing there in the dining area under the limpid light of the bulb.

Was he evil?

Was he that self-involved that he was capable of killing two young girls? I thought maybe he was. But just because he was capable of it didn't mean he'd done it. Which led me back to the question, if not him, then who? Whoever owned the sawmill? Or a couple of opportunistic drivers? Had they raped the girls? Had they raped them at the mill, let them dress and then killed them in the woods? Was it that simple?

But then what of the wet footprints, the dorm, the Russian documents...? Isaac's Canadian agent? Larry Gaynor?

I drained my glass and climbed the stairs again. I brushed my teeth in a bathroom that was a persuasive argument for suicide, part opened the bedroom window and the drapes to let in the icy air, stripped and climbed into bed.

I closed my eyes and realized I was exhausted. All my muscles sent ache-messages to my brain, and pretty soon I was drifting into deep sleep.

I was standing in Isaac's front yard. Suzy and Polly were standing in the snow, giggling, knocking at his front door. I called out to them not to go there, but they couldn't hear me, and when I tried to run my feet were too heavy, buried in the cloying drifts.

Then they had climbed the iron staircase and he was laughing, with his round, bald head shining, leading them down the corridor, opening the studio doors, saying, "Oh, you are going to *love* this!" And they were still giggling and anxiety was burning in my gut. His face was big and leering with his two front teeth missing. "Go on!" he was saying, giggling like a schoolboy, "Take your clothes off! It'll be fun! Five hundred bucks each if you'll do it!"

My heart was pounding: one, two, three...

I opened my eyes.

One, two, three... Feet on the stairs.

Instinctively I reached for my P226 under the pillow. It wasn't there. It was back in New York. Who needs a damned weapon on holiday in Maine? I cursed silently and rolled out of bed onto the floor, pulling the pillow as I went, so it lay under the duvet where I had been. I pressed up against the wall under the window, where I would be least visible, and waited.

They made no effort to be silent. Two bulky shadows filled the doorway. One of the shadows moved closer, around the wardrobe that stood against the wall, till it was beside the bed, raised its arms and a suppressed semi-automatic spat six times into the duvet and the pillow. On the sixth *phut!* I sprang.

I sprang to the foot of the bed, gripped the brass frame, jumped and kicked with both heels. It was hard to judge distance in the dark but I guess I got lucky and I caught the guy standing in the door full in the face. He went reeling into the shadows on the landing and I heard a loud crash as he hit the floor. By then I had landed behind the shooter, I had a hold of his quilted collar and, as he tried to turn to face me, I was pounding my fist into his kidneys.

The quilted jacket wasn't helping, so I leaned on his shoulder for support, jumped and smashed my right elbow down on the top of his head. I heard him grunt and felt him sag. He keeled over and knocked over the bedside table with his face. And then there were feet on the stairs. More than one pair, maybe two. I figured there were between nine and eleven rounds left—if I was lucky.

I turned, training the gun on the door. I heard muttered curses and stumbling. I guess they'd found their friend, currently doing a convincing impression of a Pekinese dog. We all waited silently for the other to make a move. While I waited I felt for my executioner's pulse. He didn't have one. It feels good to discover your executioner has no pulse.

I stood, took one long, silent stride till I was at the edge of the wardrobe, peered round and fired two shots at vague shadows hunkered down on the floor, then withdrew. I heard a sound, like a kid sucking the last of his drink through a straw. That was followed by some guttural cursing in an ugly language and then a rushing, bustling of feet. I rolled under the bed and slithered fast and silent to the far side. As I did so I heard a volley of shots hit the floor where I had been moments before. If my executioner had not been dead already, he sure as hell was now.

I came up under the window on one knee and double-tapped twice. Two shots hit the wardrobe. The other two hit a dark mass. There was a plaintive curse and then I was hit by a ten-ton truck.

It knocked the wind out of me and sent the weapon spinning under the bed. It was impossible to tell what it was. It had the mass and the weight of a large body, but at the same time I was being pounded by fists, knees, feet. As I tried to shield myself I wondered if there were more than two of them. I was pinned to the floor by the sheer weight of the mass. Knees dug into my thighs and waist. Big, hard fists pounded my shoulder and my ribs. It hurt and I knew if I let it continue I was going to die.

I tried to cover my face with my left arm and pounded savagely at his leg with my elbow. He gripped my wrist in his hand, which was what I had intended. I gripped his hand, curled forward and bit savagely at his finger, sinking my teeth deep into flesh until I felt bone. He screamed hard and pulled back. I bit harder and, as he struggled to his feet I smashed my right fist in a savage uppercut into his balls.

I got to my feet, gasping for air, and as he doubled up I mashed my knee into his face. Rage, and the fierce drive to survive was still pounding in my chest and in my head, and without thinking I wrenched the window wide open, grabbed the son of a bitch by his collar and the seat of his pants and pitched him head-first out into the snow. I switched on the light and checked the three guys, one by the bed and two in the doorway. The guy I'd kicked in the face was still alive, so I broke his neck.

Then I ran down the stairs and out into the snow. I found him in the backyard. He'd landed on his face and now, though he was lying on his belly, he was looking up at the snowflakes drifting down from the heavy clouds.

When I got back to the front door, intending to get dressed and go to the sheriff's office, I saw two headlamps turn into Water Street and move steadily down toward me. Eventually they drew level and the sheriff's Ford came to a halt. I heard the door slam and Sheriff Walt Davies came walking slowly around the hood of his truck and stood looking at me for a moment.

"You ain't cold?"

It dawned on me I was stark naked and I was freezing. "Yeah," I said. "Four guys tried to kill me and I was too busy to get dressed."

I turned and went inside. He called after me, "The neighbors heard shots and called me."

"Three of them are up in the bedroom. The other is in the backyard."

He followed me up to the bedroom and stood staring down at the three thugs as I pulled on my clothes.

"You were serious."

"Of course I'm serious."

"You did this on your own?"

"You have a big problem on your hands, Sheriff."

He wasn't listening. He crossed the room and peered out of the window, down at the crumpled mess in the backyard. "Holy shit," he said, then turned to look at me. "You are one dangerous son of a bitch."

I smiled without feeling. "It's all in the wrist action. Now, you need to listen to me, Sheriff. You have the Russian Mafia here. Suzy and Polly saw them, and they are not happy."

He closed his eyes and heaved a massive sigh.

"Don't you ever rest, Mr. Bauer? First you turn an accident into murder—an accident I warned them about! And now it's not enough that it's murder. Now it has to be the Russian Mafia!"

"I didn't turn it into murder, Sheriff. For Christ's sake wake up and smell the coffee, will you! Who do you think these guys are, for crying out loud? Check their pockets for ID, check their prints and their DNA. Maybe they're tourists looking for Jessica Fletcher's place."

"OK! OK! Quit riding me, will you?"

"Stop making like an ass and I'll stop riding you! Do your damn job for a change! There are four men here who tried to kill me. You got six shots into the damned bed. You got a guy on the floor over there with GSR all over his hand. You got two guys on the landing and one outside in the backyard, and a semi-automatic under the bed with the fingerprints of the guy with GSR on his hands. They are in my house and I am saying they tried to kill me. You want to tell me which bit of all that you do not understand? You want to explain to me how I did this?"

"OK." He raised his hands and looked around the room, shaking his head. "OK," he said again. "Why? Why do these guys want to kill you?"

I took a step toward him and fought the impulse to throw him out the window to keep company with the other guy.

"How about this, Sheriff? They want to kill me because I have been doing your job. They want to kill me because I went to the mill, found the documents written in Russian and fought with *homo Godzillicus*. He got away and went to tell his friends in Canada, who came to try and silence me before the storm stops."

He grunted. I raised my index finger. "That is *one* possible explanation."

He sighed. "Jesus," he rubbed his face again, "this is all I need."

"Yeah? It could be worse. Your daughter could be dead."

"So what the hell do I do now? We're snowed in, no radio, no telephone, no internet, and the Russian fuckin' Mafia moving in!"

"For a start, Sheriff, you bag the weapons and label them for evidence. Then get these bodies to the morgue, you print them and you get Doc Johansen to take samples for DNA which you run through CODIS as soon as you can. Then you start deputizing strong young men, you put Isaac Boothe under protective custody and you send armed men to seal off the sawmill as a crime scene, confiscate all papers and print and photograph the whole, damned place. Meantime I will go to Mathias first thing in the morning and see if we can get the cavalry to help before this whole thing goes to hell in a handcart."

As I was talking I had become aware of lights outside the front of the house, and the growing murmur of voices. I clattered down the stairs, with the sheriff just behind me, and went outside just as Hank was raising his hand to hammer on the door. Half the village seemed to be there.

"Hank—"

"Harry—"

Somebody in the crowd shouted, "We heard shots! Everybody OK?"

I stepped across the veranda. "Is Doc Johansen here?"

A woman wrapped in a quilted coat called, "He's on his way. Billy went to get him."

A man with heavy glasses, hugging his hands and stamping his feet, said, “We heard shots. Is anybody hurt?”

A woman at the back called, “I head a scream. It was horrible.”

I nodded and raised a hand. Everybody went quiet.

“There was a home invasion. Four men broke into my house and tried to shoot me.” I smiled. “Those were the shots you heard. But it has all been taken care of, so you can all go back home now.”

TWELVE

It wasn't that easy. The guy with the glasses wanted to know, "What was that scream? It was blood curdling."

Somebody else shouted, "What the hell's goin' on, Sheriff? We ain't never had violence here in Balthazar!"

A woman shouted, "What they wanna kill ya for?"

And somebody who obviously had their ear to the grapevine said, "I heard they was Russians!"

I turned and looked at the sheriff, who was wincing in the face of the unknown. He glanced at me and without thinking asked, "What do I tell 'em?"

"Get your own chestnuts out of the fire, Sheriff."

He stepped up beside me and raised both hands, like they were pointing guns at him.

"OK, listen up folks, there ain't nothing to see here, this is a case under investigation so we can make no comment at this time. Except, this is a crime scene and I need you all to stand back and go home."

"You have got to be kidding, Walt Davies."

I knew the voice and I sought her out in the crowd. It was Emma, Suzy's mother, dressed like an Eskimo, with a heavy blanket around her shoulders, and her face drawn and pale. Her husband was by her side, holding her, but he was looking at the sludge under his feet.

The sheriff said, "Now, Emma..."

But she interrupted him, cut him dead. "My daughter is dead, murdered. What Edwin said is true. We have never had violence in Balthazar, much less homicide, and now we have had two murders and one attempted murder. And you want to pat us on the ass and send us home? I'll tell you what we are going to do right now, Walt, we are going to go to the village hall, right now! And you are going to tell us exactly what is going on, who this man is, why they tried to kill him, and what is being done about it. Otherwise, you have a ton of trouble coming your way, and getting reelected is going to be the least of your worries!"

She turned and started making her way down the road toward the sheriff's office and the village hall, and the crowed turned and went with her. The sheriff leaned forward on the banister and stared down at the yellow-tinged snow.

"I don't know, I can't explain, how exactly this is your fault." He turned and looked at me. "But I know that it is."

I nodded. "I'll tell you how it's my fault, Sheriff. If I hadn't been here, nobody would have gone in search of the girls until long after any forensic evidence was gone. You would have covered up the fact that they were murdered, and those bastards at the sawmill would have continued to get away with whatever it is they are doing. But that would have been OK, because the girls would have ended up taking the blame for being careless and not taking your advice. That's how it's my fault, Sheriff. Something tells me that in your world, it is always somebody else's fault."

Hank, who had been hanging around at the foot of the wooden steps, said, "Doc's here, Sheriff."

An old Cherokee rolled down the street and crunched to a stop outside my house. Doc Johansen climbed out and stared at me for a moment like I had spoken to him in Chinese and, not only did he not understand, he didn't think it was funny.

"What's going on?"

The sheriff turned to me. "Look, I'd better go and see to this meeting. You tell the doc what it's about. I'll see you at the meeting in twenty minutes or so," he hesitated, frowning at the decking, "and, Bauer, try and back me up a bit, will you? Don't make me look bad in front of the village."

We all three watched him climb in his truck, turn around and drive away, with his headlamps reflecting black and silver on the icy blacktop. When he was gone Doc Johansen turned to me. "Before I forget," he said, "the results were negative. The girls were not raped."

Hank puffed out his cheeks. "Thank the Lord for small mercies, at least."

I sighed. "The girls were spared being raped, but it leaves a big, gaping question. Why were they killed? And the answer is looking uglier by the minute." I gestured at the front door. "We have three bodies upstairs and one out back."

The doc narrowed his eyes at me. "Bodies..."

"Yeah, dead people. Three upstairs, I threw the other one out the window."

Hank and the doc looked at each other and followed me up to the bedroom.

Twenty minutes later I left Hank helping the doctor and made my way to the complex that was the sheriff's office, the mayor's office and the village hall.

It was a large, gabled redbrick building set back among lawns which were now covered in white drifts. Thirteen white steps led up to arched heavy wooden doors that now stood open, spilling light out into the night. There was the sound of voices, some raised, some shouting. And as I made for the stairs, I saw other people approaching in twos and threes from all directions. It does not take long for the word to spread in small towns.

I looked at my watch. It was twelve o'clock, midnight. I climbed the stairs and shouldered my way through the press of people into the long hall. It was thirty or forty feet long with rows of benches either side of a central aisle. At the end there was a raised stage with a long table and four microphones set along the middle to allow the town councilors to speak louder than the people who voted for them. The sheriff was up there right now, talking to a short man in a badly cut suit who kept taking a cigar from his pocket, putting it in his mouth, glancing at his watch and putting the cigar back in his pocket. Obviously it was the wrong time to smoke a cigar.

I edged my way through the crowd as the short man with the cigar took a microphone and spoke into it.

"OK, folks, settle down now, if you'll all just take a seat we can begin... Settle down, folks, settle down now..."

Nobody took any notice and he repeated the litany again as I climbed the steps up onto the stage. He got the same response. They didn't even hear him.

I approached him, nodded, said, "Mayor," hazarding an educated guess, took the microphone from his hand and spoke into it, quietly.

"Sit down now, please." A few people turned, looked at the stage and sat. I gave it five seconds and repeated it, "Sit down now, please." People began to sit, leaving a few groups arguing at the back. I made a prolonged, quiet, "Shshshshshsh..." sound and everyone went quiet and turned to look. I pointed to the chairs. "Sit down, please. The mayor and the sheriff will say a few words, then I'll tell you what we are going to do, and after that I'll take questions."

While everybody took their seats I handed the mayor the microphone and sat on the edge of the long table. He stared at me, took his cigar out, put it in his mouth, then put it back in his pocket as he turned to speak.

"Friends," he said, and smiled. "I understand your worries and your concerns, believe me, I have daughters of my own," he simpered, "though they did not go on the March Mom March this year. But we must not let things get out of hand. It is true that since our...," he gave me a smile like curdled cream, "...our visitor has been here things seem to have been turned a little upside-down, and violence seems to have visited us for the first time in many, many decades. But the whole affair is in the very competent hands of Sheriff Davies, and as soon as the storm lets up a little we will have normal communications restored and the full support of the State Police. So please, rest assured that everything that can possibly be done, is being done." He turned to the sheriff. "Walt, I believe you had a few things to say..."

The sheriff stood and took the microphone and the mayor sat. At the back of the room I saw Rosie Jones enter with her driver. He stood by the door and she sat in the last row. The sheriff was saying:

"Folks, I am not going to double up on what the mayor has said, except to reassure you that we are doing everything that can be done. Mr. Bauer here has been the victim of a very rare and unusual violent crime, and I do not intend to let the perpetrators get away with it. Not on my watch. And I know you're all asking, well, Walt, what the hell are we going to do about it? Well, I'll tell you. For a start, we are bagging the weapons used in the attack, and anything else that might have forensic value.

"Fortunately we were able to get to Mr. Bauer's residence in time, and the bodies of his assailants are undergoing preliminary examination right now and will then be taken to the morgue. There, we will print them and Doc Johansen will take samples of their DNA. Which we will run through CODIS and AFIS as soon as we are online again. Finally, I need strong, young men to volunteer to be deputized so we can seal off the sawmill as a crime scene and thoroughly investigate it, and finally get to the bottom of what happened to *our kids!*"

There was a murmur of approval and a shuffling of backsides. They had liked what they had heard, mostly because what they had heard meant something was being done. He stood nodding at them for a moment, instinctively gauging the mood.

"So What I need you to do now, is *go home* and let us do our job. Be vigilant! Let us know if you see or hear anything suspicious, but at the same time know that we are doing everything that needs to be done. And one more thing, any able-bodied men who feel like lending a hand, come on over and see me tomorrow morning. We need deputies right now." Another murmur and the sheriff said with emphasis, "OK, folks, now *go home*."

I stood, took a couple of steps to stand beside him and put my hand on his shoulder, looking out at the crowd like we were old pals.

"Sheriff, I'd like to say a few words—"

"Oh, now Harry, I think we've said everything that needs saying. These people want to get home..."

"*Let him speak!*"

It was an imperious, authoritative voice from the back. I didn't need to look to see it was Rosie Jones. Another voice echoed her, "*Let him have his say!*" And then Emma, "*Let him speak, Sheriff, he's the only who's done anything so far! We want to know what he has to say!*"

I smiled at him and gently took the microphone from his hand.

"As you have heard, I have advised the sheriff on the next steps that need to be taken. Suzy and Polly went, on the day the storm hit, to the sawmill looking for help. They were abducted from that place, taken in a truck and murdered. I have just a few minutes ago had confirmation from Doc Johansen that Suzy and Polly were not raped."

I paused and a heavy silence fell on the room.

"That is a small consolation, but it raises two very serious questions. Why were they abducted from the sawmill? And why were they killed? We do not know the answers to those questions —*yet*. But one thing becomes very clear: that sawmill is a dangerous place, and I want to stress to all of you not to go there unless it is in a posse of armed men. Let me stress that: the sawmill poses a mortal risk to anyone who approaches it.

"Tomorrow early in the morning I am going to take the sheriff's RAM and I am going to drive to Machias to inform them of the situation we have here and ask for help. Meantime, as you have heard, the sheriff is asking for volunteers to deputize, so you can go to the mill as soon as the weather allows, close the place down and bring in the crime scene investigators to gather forensic evidence. I would strongly urge all able-bodied men in this town to do this for your wives, your daughters and the safety of your homes. Any questions?"

"Yes!" It was Rosie at the back. "Who put you in charge? Why isn't the sheriff taking care of this?"

There was a ripple of laughter. I arched an eyebrow and smiled at the sheriff.

"The sheriff is very much in charge, Rosie. I am simply consulting and helping out because I have a lot of experience in search and recovery, and conducting operations in the snow. But rest assured, your sheriff is running the show with the same skill and efficiency he has always demonstrated."

A man raised his hand. "Is it true you just killed four men who broke into your house?"

I heard the sheriff clear his throat but cut in before he could take the microphone back.

"The matter is under investigation so there isn't much I can tell you, but four men did break into my house tonight intending to shoot me in my bed. That didn't seem to me to be a great idea. So I killed them instead."

Somebody muttered, "Badass!" and everybody laughed. Somebody else called out, "I feel safer with you in town, Mr. Bauer. Can't the sheriff got to Machias and you lead us to the mill?"

There was some laughing and cheering. I handed the microphone back to the sheriff and everybody started talking, getting to their feet and shuffling toward the door. The sheriff tried to say something, but shut his mouth and handed the microphone to the mayor. He looked at me bitterly.

"I asked you not to make me look bad..."

"I didn't make you look bad, Walt. You do that all by yourself. You want to know what your big mistake is? You think people are stupid and you can manipulate them. But they're not stupid, and what they can see straight away is that I am trying to save them, but you are trying to save your professional ass."

I had spotted Emma moving through the crowd toward the stage. I excused myself from the sheriff and went down to meet her. Just behind her were her husband and Rachel, the girl I had spoken to on the first day at the lake. Emma hurried to me and gripped my hands.

"Are you all right, Mr. Bauer?"

"Harry," I said. "My name is Harry, and I am fine." I looked over her shoulder and nodded. "Ned, Rachel."

Ned cleared his throat. He was having trouble looking me in the eye. "I guess we should have taken your advice, Harry."

"Don't beat yourself up. Nobody could have foreseen this."

"Still, look, we wanted to offer you our house, till this is all over. You can't stay on your own."

"I appreciate it, but I am not going to put you guys at risk. Believe it or not, I have slept in worse conditions."

Emma squeezed my hand. "I can't bear to think of you sleeping there, after all you've done."

I grinned. "Maybe I'll sleep in the jail. I think the sheriff would enjoy that."

She laughed without much humor and I was about to move away when Rachel stepped forward and touched my arm.

"Mr. Bauer? Have you got a moment?"

Emma and her husband left, and Rachel stepped in close, staring into my eyes, clutching at my arm.

"I'm afraid," she said, "I think somebody is going to try and kill me."

THIRTEEN

"Mr. Bauer!"

I looked past Rachel and saw Rosie Jones elbowing her way through the crowd toward me. To Rachel I said, "Don't go away. Stay here behind me."

"Mr. Bauer," Rosie had arrived, "did you look into the information I gave you?"

"Yes, I did."

"And?"

"Well, Miss Jones, I am not an official investigator. The sheriff is the man..."

She rolled her eyes and sighed. "Oh, let's cut the bullshit, Harry, now that no one can hear us. We both know Walt is about as much use as a water-soluble condom! You are the man that counts here. Did you go and see Isaac?"

"Yes—"

"So quit giving me the runaround. What do you think?"

I sighed. "I think he is a man with many problems, and some very dangerous friends. Do you know anything about Larry Gaynor, his Canadian buddy?"

"Not much, probably what he told you. Sells his erotic art for him. Utter rot. It's pornography plain and simple."

I nodded. "The problem I have, Rosie, is that I have nothing to tie him either to the girls, or to the mill. You heard, I have advised the sheriff to seal the mill as a crime scene and get the crime scene officers in to scour the place, maybe they'll find a link. But so far Isaac is nothing more than a rather unpleasant man."

She snorted. "You have somewhere to stay tonight? You can't possibly stay alone in that house. I can fix you up a room at my place." There was a sparkle in her eye. "I live down the road from your friend Helen, at The Poplars. And I have Mongo to protect us."

I smiled and arched an eyebrow. She gave a small laugh. "Not, apparently, that you need protecting."

"We all need protecting, Rosie, even Mongo. Which is why I am going to decline your offer. I don't want to expose you to any risk. In any case, I doubt there are any more bad guys in Balthazar tonight."

She gave me a lopsided grin and shook her head. "You're too good to be true, Harry. Where were you, fifty years ago when I was falling in love with Isaac?" She saw my frown and laughed. "Oh, I know what he's like now! Burned out by the drugs. His teeth are falling out because the drugs and the alcohol have consumed all his calcium. He has that bald, shiny round head and that hysterical, almost effeminate manner. But you should have seen him back then. He was a firebrand, a wild, fearless adventurer exploring new frontiers of the mind. He was electrifying."

She sighed and a terrible sadness came over her face. "I can't imagine what it must be like for him, to have *been* all that, and become...," she gestured in the general direction of his house, "... *this!*"

"It must be hard," I said.

"Yes. Poor Isaac." She smiled and touched me lightly on the chest. "Well, keep me in the loop. If you change your mind I have a house on Cooper Street, a five-minute walk from here. Ask anyone, they'll tell you, and just show up. You'll be welcome."

"Thank you."

The hall was almost empty by now. For a moment her eyes fell on Rachel, who was standing slightly behind me. She smiled at her, then turned and walked away. I watched her until she had left, then turned back to Rachel. "What makes you think somebody wants to kill you, Rachel?"

She glanced around. "Is there somewhere we can go?"

"Where are your parents?"

"They didn't come." My frown made her sigh. "Some neighbors came round saying Emma was forcing a meeting at the village hall. There had been an attempt on your life and so on. They were afraid and didn't want to go out. I said I'd stick with Emma and Ned and they agreed to let me come."

"Emma and Ned have gone."

"I know, but I need to talk to you about what happened that day at the lake..." She trailed off, staring into my face. "About what I saw."

"What did you see, Rachel?"

"I don't want to talk about it here. I don't feel safe."

"I need to take you with your parents."

"No!"

I frowned at her and she glanced over at the sheriff and the mayor, still on the stage behind me.

"OK, go and wait on the stairs outside. I'll join you in a moment."

She left and I made my way back down the aisle to look up at the sheriff and the mayor. The mayor started talking.

"Young man, I want to express..."

I didn't have time so I cut him short.

"Thank you, Mayor." I turned to the sheriff. "Walt, I'll be at your office at six AM. If that RAM isn't there, I'm going to come and drag you and Hank out of bed."

He studied me with distaste. "Hank will be there with the truck. He says he wants to accompany you. I think it's a good idea."

I nodded and left. Rachel was waiting for me on the steps,

stamping her feet, clapping her hands and breathing large plumes of condensation. She followed me down the steps. "Where can we go?"

"I have to take you home. We can walk slow and you can tell me what's on your mind. But you cannot come back to my place."

"Why not? I'd feel safe with you."

We were on the path and I stopped to face her. "In the first place because tomorrow there would be a lynch mob out looking for me. All we need, with the mood the town is in right now, is people spreading rumors about me spending the night with a fifteen year-old—"

"Seventeen!"

"Fine, it makes no difference. It would be a scandal in the town, it would cause you no end of trouble and there are plenty—not least Sheriff Walt Davies—who would see it as evidence that I was some kind of pervert and it was me who killed Suzy and Polly."

"That's ridiculous!"

I nodded and started walking. She followed. I said, "So is the idea of you staying in my house, for at least another four years. And aside from that, four men just died there, and believe me, it is not a nice place to be."

Her voice took on a whining tone. "But what am I going to do? I am afraid they are going to kill me, and if I stay at my parents' house they'll kill them too. I am really scared, Mr. Bauer."

I sighed. "OK, Rachel, let's start right there. What did you see that makes you so sure they, whoever they are, want to kill you?"

We walked slowly, in the general direction of the bridge and the town center.

"We'd all been arguing about what to do. The general consensus was that we should stay put and somebody would come to get us. But Suzy and me, and Polly, all thought the storm was going to get worse and we should try to get home. But Steve, he was one of the guys, had done some survival courses and he said with no hot drinks and not enough warm clothes, some of us might get hypothermia, and that was serious."

"He was right."

"Right, so Suzy and me said we were fit and healthy, we should go ask the sawmill for help. Or if there was no one there, they'd have a landline so we could call the sheriff. Anyhow, so Polly said she'd go too, and I went to put some extra socks on and by the time I was done, they had already gone ahead. So I went after them to try and catch them up."

"OK, so what happened?"

"It was pretty slow going, and I didn't catch up to them till they were nearly at the mill. We were at the tree line, and we saw a truck coming up the road, across the clearing, coming up from the south. I figure now that it was coming from Canada along the 191, but it might have been coming from Balthazar or Machias. That road leads to an intersection in the forest, so it can lead anywhere."

"OK, so what happened."

She stopped again, in a pool of yellow lamplight, as though she was reluctant to get wherever she thought we were going.

"Suzy was about to run out and hail them, as if they could give us a ride back to town, but I felt suddenly afraid and held her arm, and told her not to."

"Why were you afraid?"

"I can't explain it. I don't know. It was something about the truck. It looked dark and dirty and ugly, and I had never seen a truck like that around here before. It's stupid and it makes no sense, but that was what I felt. Suzy and Polly got mad at me and told me not to be stupid, but I begged with them to leave it. They took no notice and next thing the gate was opening, the truck was going inside and Suzy and Polly were running across the clearing shouting for them to wait."

"Why haven't you told anyone this before?"

"Because Mom and Dad told me not to. They said it would

get us all into trouble. But I think I need to tell you and the sheriff. And I am scared."

"What happened after that?"

"The gate stayed open and I watched Suzy and Polly go inside. I could hear Suzy's voice, talking, but I couldn't make out what she was saying. Next thing the gate was closing. I began to panic."

"The fence was just chicken wire, could you see...?"

She was already nodding. "I ran a bit closer and lay down in the snow. Through the fence I saw the truck pull up outside some buildings. The back opened and there were men, I'm not sure how many, maybe ten or something like that, who came out of the building and they were carrying guns. Then women started to climb out and they were kind of herded into the nearest building. Some of them were crying, others were hugging each other. It made me really afraid.

"But the worst thing was two more men appeared, like they had come from the gate, and they had Suzy and Polly, and they were pointing guns at them."

"Could you see any of the men's faces?"

"Not really. They all had hoods and hats. I remember there was one guy who was huge, like a gorilla, but the rest, I couldn't say."

"How many women were there?"

"I think about twelve, but it might have been more. Anyhow, a couple of vans came round. They had chains on their wheels. The women were shoved into the vans and the vans drove out of the gate and headed back down the road where they had just come. At that point I just panicked and while I hoped no one was looking, I jumped up and ran."

"Who else have you told about this?"

"No one—well, Mom and Dad."

"So what makes you think they know you saw them?"

"Because I keep thinking I might have been seen."

"If they had seen you, you wouldn't be here now."

"Unless they are not sure who I am. But they might be working it out. And I don't know whose side..."

She trailed off.

"Whose side what, Rachel?"

"Whose side the sheriff is on. He doesn't pay me much heed, Mr. Bauer, but if it starts to register in his head that I went after Suzy and Polly, and those boys keep telling him they saw a third girl..."

"It won't be long before they put two and two together." I sighed. "What the hell am I going to do with you?"

"I'm sorry to cause you so much bother—"

"Don't be silly." I said it absently, with my mind suddenly elsewhere. The last stragglers were climbing in their cars and driving slowly home over the shiny, slippery blacktop, and it occurred to me that I had not seen Helen. It was possible that nobody had spread the word to her about the impromptu village meeting, but that struck me as strange. And that was when I noticed a set of headlamps silhouetting a vehicle outside my house, less than two hundred yards away down Water Street. They were silhouetting it, not hiding it, which meant the car was facing the other way, and had approached my house from the direction of the town. I took Rachel's arm and started to walk toward my house.

As we approached I saw a figure emerge from the house. Had Hank and the doc left the door open? I had hardly been in the house since I'd arrived, but thinking back I recalled the door did not lock automatically on closing. In these towns the doors were always open. I smiled grimly to myself—otherwise how would your neighbors and paid assassins get in?

We were less than a hundred yards away and trying not to lose our balance when I saw the figure open the car door. I shouted.

"*Hey!*"

My voice carried in the silence and the figure stopped and looked. A woman's voice:

"Harry?"

Helen. "Hold up!" To Rachel I said, "Come on, skate, try not to fall."

She came toward us, grabbed me. "Harry! What happened?" She glanced at Rachel. "Rachel, what are you doing here? What's going on, Harry? I heard..."

"Not now, Helen. I need you to listen very carefully. Rachel may be at risk and her parents can't protect her." I hesitated and sighed. "And I just don't trust the sheriff. I know it's a lot to ask, Helen, but can you take her in for tonight? I'll be there."

She faltered for a moment, then said, "Of course!" She opened the rear door of her car and bundled Rachel in. "But what about your parents?"

I answered, climbing behind the wheel. "I'll contact them in the morning."

Helen climbed in beside me and slammed the door, closing out the freezing night. I spun the wheel and turned the truck through a hundred and eighty degrees. Helen spoke quietly.

"I was worried about you."

I glanced at her. "I think for tonight we're OK. There were four guys and they all came for me. I guess the big gorilla told them I was tricky. But I can't imagine they sent more than four guys to the town."

"They said you killed them all."

"Who told you that?"

"Mrs. Browne. She and her husband came to tell me there was a village meeting on. They got to me late because I'm outside town. By the time I got there I saw it was already breaking up. So I went to your house. Did you kill them all, Harry?"

"Yeah." And after a moment, "They knew where I lived, and they knew what room I was in."

Nobody answered me, and we drove on in silence toward Helen's house. Nobody followed us.

FOURTEEN

Helen dropped me at the sheriff's office at five fifty-five AM. Hank was already there with the RAM, idling and melting sludge outside, sending big plumes of exhaust down the street. The snow was falling heavy and steady. Hank came out and climbed behind the wheel and I got in beside him. The sheriff stood on the steps and watched us without expression.

The big supercharged V8 growled and we pulled away, rolling steadily toward the Stony Lake Road. Even with the massive engine and the chains, progress was slow, and once we were outside town, with the wind and snow sweeping in off the frozen lake on our left, we had to stop several times, get out of the truck and shovel away the snow. It was a little over six miles from Balthazar to Machias, and it should have taken no more than ten minutes to cover the distance, but after a quarter of an hour we had progressed only a mile, the world had turned a pale gray, the snow was falling heavily and visibility was down to forty or fifty yards. Pretty soon the snow was covering the road almost as fast as we could shovel it away.

Eventually, with Hank at the wheel creeping forward, and me shoveling snow as fast as I could, we came to the top of a rise and a bend in the road. Now the road dropped at a slight incline, and a low hill rose up on our left, obscuring the lake from view. That, and the thick pine forest that covered the hill, had protected the road and I was able to climb in the cab and rest my back and arms.

Even so, with only a light dusting over the blacktop, we had to crawl, trying not to skid and slide on the black ice that covered the asphalt. Crawling, skidding and gently sliding we managed to cover another quarter of a mile, but as we approached the bottom of the slope I noticed two objects partly obscured by the snow at either side of the road.

"Stop!"

We kept going and I turned to Hank. He was frowning at me. "Why?"

"Stop, goddammit!"

We started to slew sideways. Hank was spinning the wheel, frantically trying to rectify. "I'm trying!"

But gravity and ice had taken over and we were out of control, slowly spinning on our axis as we gathered speed. He hit the bank, ricocheted and skidded across the road ass-first, where we rebounded off the bank there, scattering the drift in a big cloud of white before diving, hood first, into a huge drift that smothered our windshield.

Hank yelled, swore and pounded the wheel with his fist. I cut him short with, "Have you got a spare gun?"

"*What?*"

"*A spare gun, Hank!*" I hissed. "*Have you got one?*"

He stared at me like I was nuts. "Have I...? No! We're stuck in the..."

"Shut up and give me your gun!"

"*What?*"

"Give me your fucking gun!"

Suddenly he looked scared. But it was too late. The figure loomed behind him in his window. I reached for Hank's holster. The figure wrenched open Hank's door, grabbed a fistful of his jacket and dragged him out. The leather holster slipped through my fingers. Then the door behind me opened and two sets of powerful hands grabbed hold of me and dragged me out into the freezing snow. I fell flat on my back and next thing there were boots kicking me and stamping on me as I rolled and tried to cover my head. I was aware that in one, small way, I had the advantage: I was already on the ground, so I could not fall over. They, on the other hand, were standing on ice-covered blacktop.

I scrambled, rolled on my back—I only needed ten inches or a foot. As I hit the snow I saw four unsteady legs trying to run after me. I let them get close, rammed my elbows to the ground, pulled both knees up to my chest and smashed my heels into the nearest tibia, a quarter of an inch below the patella.

The scream was blood curdling, followed by the kind of blasphemous cursing that would have the bishop blushing and reaching for the dictionary. So I kicked again, at the same spot, and he hit the ground weeping. It was as I was struggling to my feet that I heard the click. I looked up and saw the black hole at the center of the barrel of a Ruger Super Redhawk in 454 Casull.

"Freeze!"

I grinned. "That's funny."

"Get up."

"You're not Russian," I said, as I levered myself carefully to my feet. "Are all your Russians dead?"

He didn't react. He just waved me over to the right with the revolver. As I moved away from the truck two more guys appeared around the trunk, dragging a beaten and bleeding Hank. His pistol was still in his holster. The guy with the .44 said, "Take him to the bus." Then he stepped over to the guy with the broken leg, said, "Sorry, we can't take you," and shot him in the head.

I smiled at him for the second time. "Nothing like getting people to do your work for you. How's Godzilla? He was limping last time I saw him."

"Shut up."

We clambered over the six-foot drift at the side of the road and found, about thirty yards away, between the bank and the frozen lake, a van that had caterpillars, instead of wheels. The first thing that came into my mind was if I could steel it, it would get me to Machias. The guy with the Dirty Harry revolver shoved me down the slope and said, "Get in the front passenger seat."

As I did so they shoved Hank in the back and his two captors got in either side of him and pulled semi-automatics. They didn't train them on him. They trained them on me as I climbed in. Then the guy with the revolver got in behind the wheel. He looked at me for a second.

"I know who you are, Harry Bauer. I know you are a very dangerous man and I am not going to underestimate you. If you do anything unexpected, move too suddenly, anything at all, they will kill the deputy instantly and then they will shoot you. We would like to take you alive, but we don't need to. So sit still and be smart until we get to our destination."

He was convincing and I thought, for the moment, it was probably good advice.

We set off at speed along the edge of the lake. We were doing maybe thirty miles an hour, but over deep snowdrifts and countryside it was enough to be an uncomfortable ride. We covered the distance back to the outskirts of town in a couple of minutes, then veered off the lakeside and onto the frozen water. I looked at the driver.

"This is a lot of weight for new ice."

"You think? I guess we're about to find out, huh?"

He hit the gas and I guess we must have covered the half-mile stretch in less than a minute. It was when we were about halfway across, and I could begin to make out the far shore through the falling snow, that I realized we were headed directly for Isaac's house.

I studied the driver's face for a moment. There wasn't much to learn there so I asked him, "Are we going to meet the boss?"

He did something that should have been a smile but wasn't.

"You ain't gonna meet the boss."

We hit the shore to the north of the houses and then began to climb more slowly through the forest, following what was probably a track but was now just a snowy space between tall trees.

We were going north and east and it was clear we were making for the mill. That gave me a spark of hope. If it was just these three guys and the sheriff turned up with a posse, we might just get out of this and make a useful arrest.

He must have read my mind, because he glanced at me and gave me another one of his unpleasant smiles.

"Forget it, Bauer. Sheriff Walt Davies ain't coming, and the 7th Cavalry are otherwise engaged. It's gonna be just you and me, and a few friends. Personal and intimate, like."

I nodded, but I didn't answer. I was aware they hadn't bothered to cuff me. They had by now taken Hank's weapon, but whichever way you looked at it, they were confident. Way too confident given what the driver had said about not underestimating me, just a few minutes earlier.

Progress had become slower since we had entered the forest, but after about five minutes we joined the track that led across the clearing to the mill. The gate was open and we drove right in to stop in front of the office building where I had found the documents written in Russian. The driver killed the engine and studied my face a moment.

"Get out," he said. "If you try to run we will kill the deputy, then we'll go after you."

I climbed out and noticed, in the parking lot beside the office, a truck adapted to the snow and four snowmobiles.

The rear passenger doors opened and the two guys in the back dragged Hank out and dumped him in the snow. He was bleeding from his nose and his mouth, and from a gash on his head.

"This man needs a doctor."

The guy with the revolver shrugged. "Pretty soon he'll need an undertaker, if we don't get our shit together. You want I should shoot him now an' put him out of his misery? Then we'd have to cuff and manacle you, maybe break your leg like you did to Pete and Zoli."

I shook my head. "What do you want from me?"

"I want you to get inside and climb the stairs, and quit wasting time."

I made my way toward the office door with the driver just behind me. I heard them drag Hank to his feet and wondered how bad off he really was, or whether he was laying it on thick to lull them into a false sense of security. They taught you to do that in the Regiment. But after a moment's thought I decided Hank was a good man and tough, but not that subtle. He'd taken a sound beating and he was out for the count. I opened the door and climbed the stairs.

On the landing I stopped. There were four guys there. They were big and they looked mean. Two were leaning either side of the office door. The one on the right was bald and had a baphomet tattooed on his head. His pal had a big, Attila the Hun moustache. The other two were in one of the other offices and came out into the passage as I climbed the stairs. One of them was young and skinny, no more than twenty, with crazy blue eyes and blond hair that flopped over his face. The fourth had Russian Special Forces written all over him, with hair cut so short you could see his scalp and long, powerful limbs. With the three guys behind me that made a total of seven.

The voice behind me said, "In the office."

I went in and they brought Hank in after me and dumped him in the chair behind the desk. The guy with the Redhawk shoved the other chair at me and said, "Sit."

As I sat he perched himself on the corner of the desk, looking down at me.

"My name is Larry," he said.

"Gaynor?" He nodded. "You sell Isaac's erotic art for him."

"Are you telling me or asking me."

"I'm just trying to impress you with my knowledge."

His blank face told me I wasn't cutting the mustard.

"This can go one of two ways, Bauer. It can be easy, and you might even get to go home, or it can be hard." He smiled. "Now, when you think that going home is only a possibility the easy way, that is going to give you some idea of what the hard way is like."

I nodded for a bit before answering. Then I said, "You don't need to sell it to me, Larry. I saw what you did to the girls. What do I need to do to be able to go home? This isn't my fight. I'm supposed to be on holiday."

He did something that was too quiet to make it to a chortle.

"You're here on holiday."

"Yeah."

"So why'd you come snooping around here, poking your nose into shit that doesn't concern you?"

I shrugged and made a "what can I tell you" face. "I'm basically a good guy. I like to help. I knew the kids were going to be in trouble so I lent a hand. When the girls showed up dead, I assumed they had been raped, killed and dumped. The fact they hadn't been raped only became apparent after they had thawed out. By that time, you had already sent your boys to try and kill me." I shook my head. "I only discovered I was out of my depth way after it was too late."

He grunted. "So we have a problem."

I gave a short laugh. "I have a problem. Which is why I am asking you, what do I have to do to make this go away? I don't want to die, and I am willing to work hard to stay alive."

He leaned back and laughed. It wasn't a big, booming belly laugh, but it was a laugh of real amusement. I might have told an amusing, relevant anecdote about the president, or a recent Oscar winner while at a dinner party.

When he was done he shook his finger at me in the negative. "No," he said. "You're very good, but no. I don't believe you. The timing is too perfect. I think you're either with the Feds, or the DEA."

"The timing..."

"Also, I did a search for Harry Bauer of Manhattan, New York, and pal, you are not on any databases."

"That's not so hard to do, you know that."

"Oh, sure," he nodded, "but why would you want to?"

"What can I tell you, after eight years in the British SAS I am not crazy about Islamic fundamentalists or South American cartels being able to look me up on Google and drop by to put a bullet through my head. I'm weird that way."

He was thoughtful for a moment. Then, "It's not such a strange progression, SAS, FBI or DEA."

I barked a single laugh. "Are you kidding me? In the first place the FBI would drive a Blade nuts. The Regiment is all about *self*-discipline. We discuss our missions with our officers, they don't tell us what to do. We are experts in our own right. I wouldn't last a week in the Feds. They'd drive me nuts and I'd drive them nuts. Besides, I was discretely drummed out. I was invited to resign and was *not* honorably discharged. I applied to the Feds and the DEA when I was getting desperate, they both turned me down."

He glanced over at the diabolical bald head and nodded. The bald baphomet left, presumably to check on my story. That was a good thing.

Gaynor looked down at his thumb like he was trying to polish it. "So," he said after a while, "when the Bureau and the DEA turned you down, what job *did* you get? You are a very wealthy man. Where does all this wealth come from?"

I sighed and thought about it for a slow count to five. Then I looked him in the eye and said, "I'm a hit man."

FIFTEEN

"You're a hit man." He nodded a few times, smiling a dangerous smile at the floor. "So who sent you?"

I shook my head. "I'm on holiday."

He frowned. It was a curious, inquisitive frown. "Do you expect me to believe that?"

I shrugged. "I don't give a damn if you believe it or not. If I cared I would have lied and told you I invested the money I stole from drug dealers in Colombia. But the truth is I'd done a few hits and I was burnt out. So I took a vacation in the quietest, most remote part of the USA."

He sat in silence for a while, staring at me, chewing his lip. Eventually I asked him, "Why'd you kill the girls?"

"I didn't. If I'd been here we would have found another way of dealing with it." He sighed, slow and deep and stared at the door, like a different way of dealing with the problem was lingering there, like a ghost of solutions past. "They'd just taken a delivery of women, the girls saw it." He spread his hands and turned back to me. "How do you explain to two seventeen-year-old girls why you have a truck full of women, half of them sobbing their eyes out, the other half with bruises and black eyes?"

"How do you explain that to anyone?"

He smiled. "How would I explain it to a paid killer? I'd say 'It's life, and life gets ugly sometimes.' To a cop I'd say, 'You didn't see anything, and here's ten grand. Go buy your wife a dress and your kids some toys. And by the way, I know where you live.' To the mayor I'd say, 'Here's twenty grand, and if you get smart I'll send Harry Bauer to throw you headfirst out of the *fucking window!*'"

The last two words he roared and his face went red. I counted slowly to five while he glared at me, then I smiled. "I like the mayor's explanation. Why don't you explain it to me like that?"

"I'd like to." He stood and went to the door, stood staring out at the landing. "Truly," he said, and turned to look at me, "I am a diagnosed sociopath. I don't understand empathy. I don't care if you suffer, if a small child suffers, if a little bunny rabbit suffers. It just doesn't affect me. But I am a businessman, and I do know that when people cooperate, things get done and money gets made. So what I would like, is to save myself the trouble of disposing of two more bodies, save myself the trouble of cleaning up the mess after torturing you both," he looked over at Attila the Moustache and laughed, "I mean, fucking wooden floors, right?" Attila laughed. "You remember? It took fuckin' days to get the blood and the vomit out of that floor. You remember that?"

Attila had a voice like tectonic plates in collision. "Remember?" he said. "I spent a week scrubbin' those boards with bleach! In the end I had to pull 'em up and replace 'em."

"OK, Larry, you made your point. What do I need to do so you won't spend a week scrubbing me and Hank off the floorboards?"

He didn't answer straight away. He stared at me with his eyebrows slightly raised, and eventually he said, "You have to tell me who sent you."

"OK." I thumped the arms of my chair gently with the heels of my hands. "I can lie to you and tell you that the CIA Special

Activities Center has employed me to come and eliminate you or Isaac Boothe. My activities since I have been in this godforsaken town would make no sense, the fact that I have brought no weapons with me would make no sense, and the fact that I have spent my time trying to rescue girls instead of hitting my targets would *make no sense!*" I paused. "But I can tell you that if that is what you want to hear. But the *fact* is that I am burned out and I needed a holiday."

"People on holiday usually go to Miami or Hawaii. Who comes to a dump like this?"

"People who are tired and prefer trees and country walks to assholes in shorts, jungle shirts and Havaianas, drinking piña coladas."

He seemed to think about it for thirty seconds, then looked at Attila and said, "Tie him to the chair. And Hank."

I went to stand. "*Now wait a minute!*" But six semi-automatics pointing at me kept me in my chair. They used duct tape and bound my wrists to the arms of the chair and my ankles to the legs. When Attila was done, Larry came and leaned over me, with his face just a couple of inches from mine. "We are going to go down now, get some coffee, snort some coke, get stoked. When we come back—it might be ten minutes, half an hour, tonight, who knows?—but when we come back I am going to want a convincing explanation for why you are here. If I don't get it, I am going to dismember Hank one joint at a time. And when I am done, I am going to dismember you. So you had better do some pretty smart thinking while I'm gone."

He smiled and patted my cheek, and I decided for that alone I was going to have to kill him.

The door closed and I heard the key turn in the lock. Then there was the sound of voices and feet tramping down the stairs.

Duct tape is not so hard to get free from if you have some way to just nick the edge. Then it will split real easy. But they had bound my hands tight and I could not move them an inch. I thought about inching the chair across the room to the desk and trying to scrape the edge of the tape against the edge of the desk. But the edge of the desk looked too smooth, and they had bound my ankles so tight I could barely move my feet. Besides which the scraping of the chair would be audible downstairs. To make matters worse, I didn't know whether I had ten minutes or six hours.

I became aware of Hank looking at me. His pupils were dilated and his mouth was sagging open.

"Are they gonna kill us, Harry?"

"No, Hank."

He tried to smile. "They hurt me pretty bad. They wouldn'a got you if it wasn't for me. You would'a killed 'em all."

"We ain't done yet, Hank."

"You don't worry 'bout me, Harry. Y'hear? I'm all in. You get outta here and get help. Don't worry about me."

Beside me, maybe six inches to my right, was the filing cabinet from which I had taken the files. I had closed the drawer, but I had not locked it, and now it stood open half an inch. I stared at it and wondered. Crossing a room was one thing, shifting a mere six inches was another.

I angled my toes to the right as far as they would go, straining hard enough that I almost got cramp in my calves. Then I pressed my toes to the floor, leaned forward as far as I could and gave myself a push and swiveled my feet. Nothing happened except that I flopped back in my chair. I spent five minutes practicing and finally managed to move two inches toward the cabinet. The effort had also slightly loosened the tape around my ankles. I kept going, and after twenty minutes I had severe strain in my calf muscles and I was at a point where I could touch the open drawer with my right baby finger. For a moment I felt triumphant. Then sagged back in exhaustion as I asked myself, "Now what?"

I managed to hook my finger inside the drawer and, with extreme effort and difficulty I pulled it out maybe half an inch, and then, hooking my finger inside and gripping tight, I pulled myself an inch closer, so the raw edge of the metal drawer was resting against the tape. Now I was getting somewhere.

That was when the door opened, and Larry stood smiling at me with that unpleasant smile.

"I guess you've been thinking about the wrong thing."

I sighed and closed my eyes. "Larry, whatever I tell you is going to be a fabrication..."

"Stop. I've had enough of your bullshit." He leaned back. "Get the pliers. No, the small, pointed ones. Make it hard," he looked at me, "so we have to pull and tear a bit. This is on you, Bauer."

"For Christ's sake, Gaynor! He's delirious. Can't you see he's dying? There is no point—"

"Shall we take your fingers off instead? You're not delirious yet?"

"There is no need to do this! I am telling you the truth!"

Attila and the young skinny kid came in. The skinny kid was giggling, excited. He grinned at Gaynor and wiped his nose with the back of his hand. "Can I do it? I never done it before."

Hank was looking at me and had started to sob. I shouted, "OK! Stop! I'll tell you!"

Gaynor ignored me and handed the kid the pliers. "OK, but cut through the bone, not the cartilage in the joint. The bone hurts like eighty percent more." He turned to me. "What?"

"I'll tell you, but let Hank go. He has no part of this."

He laughed. "Let the deputy go?" He shook his head, laughing again. "No, you don't understand. *Hank*, the deputy, dies. We either torture him to death, or he dies a fast, painless death. But, come on, Bauer, how can we let the sheriff's deputy go?"

"You bought the sheriff, didn't you? Pay Hank off too."

"We didn't buy off the sheriff, he looks the other way and we don't kill his family. It's a tacit agreement, nothing more."

My voice was beginning to rise and there were hot coals burning in my belly. "So make the same, tacit agreement with Hank! He'll look the other way!"

"Why would I, Bauer? It's a risk, a loose end, especially after he turns up half brain dead looking like he was mauled by a bear!"

"Let him go and I will tell you everything. Torture him and I will tell you *nothing!* Kill him and I will tell you *nothing!*"

His eyebrows rose high on his forehead and I knew I had made a mistake. "Wrong answer, Bauer."

He raised the Redhawk. I shouted some inarticulate plea and the gun exploded. The impact of the .44 slug imploded Hank's chest and erupted out of his back, driving him hard against the safe.

"Now, Mr. Bauer, we get to find out whether you will tell us nothing or everything. Dave," he turned to the skinny kid, "I think we'll start with the baby finger on his left hand."

Dave craned his neck toward the door. Attila laughed and leaned out, "Hey! Dave gonna take off this guy's fingers. He never done it before. He wants you to watch. Come on!"

There was the sound of scraping chairs, grunts, a little laughter, and I was suddenly aware of a deep, almost insane hatred located inside my chest and my belly. It was hot, it was red and it was fermenting. I looked at Dave, searching for some humanity in him, but found none. As the others came in, crowding round the door and grinning at Dave, I began to roar. It was a crazy, frenetic screaming roar as I gripped the drawer with my right baby finger and rocked the chair and the filing cabinet back and forth, pounding them against the wall in a frenzy. To them it must have looked like the amusing frenzy of panic of a helpless man facing agonizing torture. To me it was a last-ditch, desperate attempt to get one, small tear in the tape around my wrist.

Dave's face came up close and he yelled at me like I was being unreasonable.

"Hey, cut it out!"

I stopped, my heart pounding high and hard in my chest.

Everyone stared hard, their jaws slack, as he fitted the small, sharp plier, which ended in a cruel, pointed beak, to my finger, taking care get the bone and not the cartilage. His pale blue eyes locked onto mine and he began to squeeze. The pain was like nothing I had ever experienced before. I wrenched my arm up and away and the masking tape tore where I had made the nick. The pliers hung from my finger where they had bitten into the bone, with blood oozing down. I flipped them. They came loose and I gripped the handle, and in a fraction of a second I had rammed them into the top of Dave's head. His eyes rolled up and his jaw dropped. I wrenched them out again and he just seemed to wobble like a lobotomized Jell-O.

It was less than a second, and Attila was rushing at me, with his arms reaching for my throat. It was a bad move because the pliers went straight in his left eye. He screamed hysterically. I wrenched them out again and, while he blocked access to me I slashed at the tape on my ankles and my left wrist.

As I stood Attila was just inches away from me, still screaming and clutching at his eye. There were hands gripping at his shoulders and his side, trying to move him aside so they could get at me. I thought I'd oblige and, with the open pliers, I cut deep into the side of his neck, severing the carotid and the aorta, then spun him round so he was spraying his lifeblood all over his pals. Meanwhile I snatched the Glock he had stuffed in the back of his waistband, kicked Baphomet hard in the thigh and lunged for the door. Hands grabbed at me but I made it out to the landing and, without thinking, vaulted over the banisters as a hail of bullets hit the wall.

I landed awkwardly and scrambled, tumbling down the stairs. I reached the bottom running and burst out into the snow. It was coming down heavy and fast. The air was freezing and visibility was down to maybe twenty or thirty yards.

For a second I looked over at where I knew the trucks and the snowmobiles were. I had no keys and no time to hotwire them, especially with frozen fingers. So I set off at a run toward the gate, wading through the drifts as fast as I could, knowing that within minutes the freezing air would start rupturing the cells in my lungs.

I had to do something. I had to do something right then. But I had no idea what I was going to do.

SIXTEEN

What I had to do was get to Isaac's house and beat a confession out of him. The only trouble was, I was going to be dead long before I reached Isaac's place, over two miles away. Not only was I going to get lost, if I didn't die of hypothermia, I'd start coughing up blood, or, most likely, I was going to get shot.

Behind me, as I waded through the gate and onto the snowy plane before the forest, I heard wild shouts and whoops, and the roar of snowmobiles. This was going to be a hunt, and I was going to be the quarry. I needed desperately to get to the trees before they caught up with me, but struggling through the two-foot-deep snow was slowing me down to little more than a normal walking pace.

I kept my mouth shut and tried to breathe through my nose. It was hard because my lungs were screaming out for air. Behind me I heard the snowmobiles erupt from the compound. Visibility was low and at first they didn't see me. I looked back and through the mist of swirling flakes I could see their lights fanning out, slowing down, zigzagging to make sure they didn't miss me.

I turned and ran, lifting my knees high to avoid having to wade, aiming for the nearest fringe of trees maybe eighty or ninety yards away. In normal conditions it was a thirty-second sprint. But at that moment it was an impossible struggle against impossible odds. It might as well have been a thousand miles away.

I looked back and saw with a jolt of adrenaline that I had pulled ahead. They had slowed almost to a crawl. For a second I wondered why, and then it hit me. They were searching for my tracks, and if they found them before I got to the trees, I was finished. I was as good as dead.

I redoubled my efforts, but my back and my lungs were beginning to go into spasm, and the tree line was still a good seventy paces away. I figured I was doing two paces to a yard, which put me a hundred and forty exhausting paces from the forest, and I knew I was never going to make it.

A voice in my head told me not to think. Just to stare at the snow and take one pace after another. One step after another. And then I heard the shout, the whoops and the revving of the engines. I dropped on my belly and crawled furiously to my left, half-covering myself with snow as I went, describing a wide arc until I was facing back the way I had come. The engines were loud, hurtling toward the spot where I had been moments earlier, barely ten or twelve feet away. There were five of them, looking like aliens in hoods and goggles, one at the front whom I assumed was Gaynor, two behind him, and two more behind them, forming a kind of flying V.

Within seconds they were upon me, kicking up great sheets of snow. Gaynor flew past, and it must have been dawning on him right then that he had lost the tracks. The snowmobile behind him passed within six feet of me and the next was practically on a collision course. I stood and jumped to my right as I fired. The slug struck home into his chest and tore him off the seat and back into the snow. He was probably no more than three or four feet away.

I lunged for the machine. He'd let go the throttle and it slowed. I clawed at the seat, then at the handlebars and pulled myself on. There was a moment of confusion. The other four had slowed and were going in circles, trying to pick up my tracks again. They hadn't heard the shot above their engines.

I revved the engine and took off like a bat out of hell, and they were right behind me. I had a rough idea where the road was and pointed the machine in that direction. In the middle of a forest in a snowstorm, a rough idea is just about as bad as no idea at all, because the microscopic errors you keep making become exponential and pretty soon you're going in the opposite direction to where you want to go. But for now it was all I had. I was pretty sure the mill was behind me, and the road through the woods was ahead and to the left. That meant if I didn't collide with a tree, I was probably on the right track.

Then they were there, looming huge and black through the mist of snow. They were densely packed, about thirty or forty feet away. I swerved left to avoid crashing and opened up the throttle, skimming along the face of the tree line, looking for the opening. Behind me I was aware of Gaynor and his boys closing on me. Then I saw it up ahead, a gap in the trees, and I banked right and hurled myself into it, raising a great sheet of spray on my left. It must have temporarily blinded at least one of them, but they kept coming.

I knew the road. I had walked it and I had driven it. I knew there was a big bend to the right, where I had found Suzy and Polly's bodies, and I knew there was a fork on the left which was easy to miss. It was where we had come out today, and it led down to the lake right by Isaac's house.

I stayed close to the left of the road, searching for anything familiar, but in the low visibility it was hard. Because the moment you saw anything at all, it was gone.

And then it was there. If I hadn't been looking for it I would not have seen it. I braked, turned, skidded and fishtailed, keeping the revs high. I let out the clutch and hurtled into the narrower path between the trees. This track had more twists and bends, dips and humps. Behind me I could hear a chaos of shouts and revving engines. I took a bend, accelerated and flew over a small hill, landing in a vast shower of snow. Immediately after that there was a bend to the right. I stopped on the bend, took the Glock and aimed it at the hill. I could hear the straining engines growing louder, and suddenly the first of them sprang over the rise. I trailed him for one and a half seconds till I had a bead, and then I fired six rounds in rapid succession.

He hit the snow in a mess. The snowmobile bounced and twisted and his riddled body flew off like a twisted mannequin. But by that time I was accelerating away and his four pals were leaping over the hill behind him. I wondered if they would collide with him, and I wondered also if I had killed Gaynor. He had been in the lead, but it was also possible that in the confusion he had overshot and somebody else had taken the lead. I decided if they stopped coming it meant I'd shot Gaynor.

They didn't stop coming. The kept coming, relentless and obviously more experienced than me at riding snowmobiles, because they were closing on me again. It was two miles to Isaac's place, as the crow flies. With all the twists and bends it was more like three. I figured we were doing forty to fifty miles per hour. It doesn't sound fast on paper, but on a twisting forest track, in heavy snow with visibility down to twenty or thirty yards, you may as well be doing two hundred. What you see thirty yards away at fifty miles an hour, is on top of you in just one second.

I didn't know if I was on the right track. These forests were full of tracks like these. But I figured as long as I was hurtling downhill I was hurtling toward the lake, and from the lake I'd be able to see Balthazar and Isaac's house. And if I was headed for the lake, I had to be practically on it by now.

I began to be aware then of a snowmobile inching up on my right. We had hit a straight stretch and he was using it to full advantage to close the gap. We came to a hump and leapt, and when we hit the ground again he was practically level with me. I turned and saw that he had a weapon in his hand and he was trying to aim. I saw the muzzle flash, braked instinctively and saw him shoot ahead. Then I opened up the throttle to full and charged after him.

I could hear the others closing behind me, and he made the mistake of thinking they could now box me in. As he looked over his shoulder to maneuver I rammed him hard in his left side. I was probably doing sixty. His machine lurched and rolled, sending him sprawling. But my ride ricocheted to the left, sending me flying over the bank and down among the trees.

If there was a Guinness Book of Records entry for the number of times a person said, "*Shit!*" in thirty seconds, I would have won it. The trees were not jungle thick. They were probably between four and six feet apart. But it was dark in the forest and visibility was down to no more than two or three yards. The incline was steep and if I had even tried to brake I would have simply skied down the slope. At least with the engine I retained a small amount of control.

I twisted and turned and managed to take most of the collisions on the sides of the machine. I lurched over roots and humps buried in the snow, jumped over sudden hollows and ditches, skimmed past vast tree trunks and hurtled down slopes that seemed to be practically vertical. Until I swerved right to avoid a rock and found I was on the edge of a precipice. For a fraction of a second I skimmed along the edge, but then gravity took a hand and tipped me over.

Your instinct in a moment like that is to cling to your vehicle. Few people like being suspended out in the void, and most would prefer to cling to something solid. But when the solid thing you're clinging to weighs five hundred pounds and is probably going to fall on top of you, it's better to be out in the void. So I leapt.

I heard the machine crash into something solid just before I hit the snow and started to roll and slide. Then I was in midair again. Instinct made me curl and cover my head with my arms. Nothing happened for a fraction of a second. Nothing happened for another fraction of a second and I knew I was falling from a great height.

Then it happened. It was jarring, violent and left me stunned and vaguely incredulous at the amount of pain that was penetrating my whole body. I tried to roll, but I was paralyzed by the pain. I looked and saw I had hit a tree. There was a cliff, and trees leaning over the cliff like they were looking down at me. There was a lot of snow falling on my face, and I knew I had to move or I would be buried and die of hypothermia.

On my right as I lay, there was flatness. It was white and flat. The lake. I must be near Isaac's place. I tried to move again but the pain was crippling and sent shards of spasm through my lungs. A voice in my head told me to rest a moment and recover. Just a moment to recover my strength. I knew that voice would kill me if I listened to it. Its intentions were good. I knew that. It had my best interest at heart. I knew that. I knew that if it could it would wrap me up in a warm bed and bring me chicken soup. Care for me and keep me warm and safe in my bedroom in Manhattan, with a fire burning in the grate. I could see the colonel there, Jane, hunkered down tending the fire, with her nice legs and her blue suit. The brigadier was there too, and they were laughing and chatting, wagging their fingers at me. "You have to rest," that was the brigadier. Jane said, "You have to rest, darling. You know you need to."

And I did know that. Every fiber of my body knew it, and smiled and eased and relaxed as the knowledge became a certainty.

Pain shot through my chest like a stiletto stalactite piercing my lungs. I opened my eyes and despair filled my mind. Snow was falling on me out of the leaden sky and a huge face, like an alien in a hood and goggles, was leering down at me.

I closed my eyes, willing myself back to Manhattan, with Jane and the brigadier, in the warmth of my room. But strong hands gripped my legs and my shoulders and a voice said, "Get him in the truck."

The pain as they lifted me was excruciating, but brought me back to Maine with a vengeance. They shoved me in the back of a van and one man got in beside me. Two more got in the front. I was wheezing badly and the stabbing pains wouldn't stop. The next fifteen minutes were like being in hell. Every move I made was agony, but remaining still was agonizing too. We sped and rattled over the ice, through the deep, gray light, then bumped off the lake surface and up a track. Every bump and rattle was like having blades of cold glass driven through my chest, making it almost impossible to breathe.

Then I was being dragged from the truck, half carried across a blanket of snow and in through a door. There were voices talking urgently. Warmth, and I realized I was freezing and shivering. I knew I was losing control and I knew I was about to die. Somehow in that moment the ancient Norse myths came to me, and I knew it was not important to avoid death. What was important was to die well. I tried desperately to resist, to move, to get on my feet and fight.

I saw myself kicking free from the men who held me, punching, kicking, somehow wielding a sword, slashing, hacking, warm blood flowing red, fire surging, consuming the house, consuming me as I killed Suzy and Polly's killers. I was dying among the blood and fire of vengeance. And vengeance was mine.

SEVENTEEN

I OPENED MY EYES.

I heard the crackle of a fire. I was warm. The pain in my lungs had gone. I was on a sofa, and the warmth of the fire was on my right. More impressions came slowly. I had a duvet over me. My jacket had been removed and so had my shoes. I tried to move but the room rocked and made me feel seasick. I let it settle and tried again with more success.

I was in a half-sitting position, leaning on my right elbow, and saw opposite me, in an armchair and leering at me, Isaac.

"Hello, Harry Bauer."

"That was you..."

"Hard to know, really. Probably."

"In the truck, with the goggles."

He nodded, still grinning. "You may feel a bit weird for a while. I gave you a little cocktail to numb the pain and aid recovery."

"What kind of cocktail?" I snarled.

"You're welcome. Nothing your reactionary soul would object to. Protein powder and hot chicken soup. You probably don't remember that. You were delirious, and compresses of rosemary, arnica and lavender oil for the bruise."

I screwed up my face in an expression which probably looked ungrateful.

"Are you serious?"

He didn't answer the question. Instead he said, "We heard the snowmobiles going crazy and when I looked out I saw you go over the edge. So I got Chico and Nandez to come out with me in the truck. I was quite surprised when I saw it was you."

"I bet you were." I made a supreme effort and managed to get myself into a sitting position, propped against the arm of the sofa. He was watching me curiously.

"So what were you doing on a snowmobile in the forest? The last I heard you had gone on some heroic quest to far Machias in search of help and reinforcements."

I stared at him for a very long moment. "I'll tell you what I was doing, Isaac. I was on my way here, to stick a gun down your throat and force you to confess."

He glanced over behind the sofa. "Your pistol is over there, on the credenza, by the way. Confess to what?"

I laughed. It hurt and I had to stop, but laughed again in spite of the pain. "You know." I gestured with my open hand toward where I thought the forest was. "You *know* who was chasing me!"

"I didn't know anyone was chasing you, Harry."

"Come on, Isaac! You said yourself you heard the snowmobiles going crazy!"

"But I didn't know they were *chasing* you! I just told you I had no idea why you were out there."

"You *sent them to get me!*"

"You're not making a lot of sense, Harry. I didn't *send* anybody. I told you, I went with Chico and Nandez—"

"*Oh, come on!*" I shouted and the pain made me stop and hold my breath. "What the hell do you think you're playing at, Isaac?" I said more quietly. "What do you think I was talking to them about before I escaped?"

He leaned forward, with his elbows on his knees, frowning. "Talking to *whom* about, Harry? And escaped from *where?*"

I sat up with my feet on the floor. "Now you listen to me, you son of a bitch. Don't you try and pull this weird Kafka shit on me or I swear, fractured ribs or no fractured ribs, I'll come over there and—"

"I am nearly eighty years old, Mr. Harry Bauer. What will you, a trained killer, do to this old man? This old man who went out in the snow, over the frozen lake, to save your life. What will you do to me, in spite of your fractured ribs?"

I closed my eyes and flopped back against the sofa.

"OK," I said, "we'll play it your way. We were on our way to Machias when we were ambushed."

"You and who else?"

"You *know* who else..." I sighed and rolled my eyes. "Fine! Hank! Hank was with me and we were ambushed. I was able to defend myself but Hank got very badly beaten. We were dumped in a truck that had been adapted for the snow and we were taken up to the mill."

He raised his eyebrows. "To the mill, where the two girls were abducted."

"Yes, you son of a bitch! Where your men abducted and murdered Suzy and Polly. And for your further astonishment, shall I tell you who it was who abducted me, and murdered Hank in cold blood while he was sitting right in front of me? You want me to tell you?"

The grin had faded from his face and he was watching me very closely. "Yes," he said, "I want you to tell me."

"Your pal, Larry Gaynor! How much longer do we have to play this game, Isaac?" We stared at each other. I gestured with my hand toward the forest and the mill. "He told me! He told me what happened! That Suzy and Polly arrived at the mill looking for help just as they were unloading the girls. The girls were bruised and weeping, and they were loaded into a smaller truck and driven away. Obviously Suzy and Polly could not be allowed to go home, so they broke their necks and dumped them in the forest."

"Larry told you this?"

"Yeah, Larry told me this."

"That stupid asshole."

"Now you're going to tell me you didn't know about this?"

"I'm not going to tell you anything. You are a very dangerous man. The less you know the better."

My chest had started to ache and I tried to position myself in the corner of the sofa, where the pain would be less.

"Isaac, there is no way out of this. You went too far, like you always do. You killed two teenage girls, for Christ's sake."

"I didn't." His voice was simple and matter of fact. "I wasn't there. I was here at home. Chico and Nandez will swear to that."

"Oh, sure. But what happens when they get Gaynor in the interrogation room, Isaac? What happens when his counsel starts negotiating with the DA? What happens when they get you in front of a jury and you start acting and talking crazy because you can't help yourself?" He stood and walked over to the window. I kept pressuring him. "Who is going to believe that Gaynor didn't call you when the kids turned up? You are the boss of this operation—"

He turned to look at me. "Is that what you think?"

"Quit bullshitting, Isaac! It's over! You and Gaynor set this damned thing up together. You used your erotic art as a front. And I'll give you credit. It was smart. Who would use something the whole damned state disapproves of as a front? Nobody but you! Because behind that front was the exploitation of women making pornographic movies which you publish online and make a fortune out of.

"And you're telling me that when those kids showed up and saw the women being taken from the truck, the men at the mill didn't call you and ask you what to do?"

"They didn't."

"Well I guess we'll find out at trial, Isaac. You asked what I would do to an old man. You need to be asking what they would do to an old man in prison, Isaac. You need to be thinking about a confession and a plea bargain before Larry gets in there ahead of you."

He looked around the room, like he might have left a solution somewhere and wanted to find it again. "What can I do?" he said. "I didn't go and rescue you for this."

Suddenly, and in spite of myself, I felt pity for him. He moved to an old-fashioned telephone he had standing on a lamp table. He picked it up and held it to his ear. "Dead," he said simply and put it down. "I'll have to call my lawyer. But just calling my lawyer will be enough for Harvard to stop my pension. I never killed anybody."

"But the dog."

He nodded absently, staring out at the snow. "Yes, the dog."

I sat up again and looked at the window. It was dark outside. "How long have I been here?"

"Six hours." He frowned at me. "Do you think I killed the girls? Do you think I looked into their eyes as I killed them?" He shook his head. "I couldn't have. I was here. I was here all day. The snow. I couldn't go out."

Six hours. I wondered what the hell had happened during those six hours. What had Gaynor been doing? Had they brought me here for some reason? Why hadn't they killed me? The phone lines were down and cell and radio coverage was not working because of the storm. So maybe they were not in touch. Maybe Gaynor didn't know I was here.

"Where is Gaynor, Isaac?"

"I don't know."

"Does he know I'm here?" He shrugged, still staring at the window. Then shook his head. "No. How could he?"

"Are you in touch?"

He pointed at the window. "In this?"

"Did you know he was here?"

He lowered himself in the chair. The crackling of the fire seemed very loud in the silent room. "He comes and goes." He looked at me. "You know? He doesn't always tell me."

"How does it work? The erotic film thing?"

He spread his hands. "I get an inspiration. I want it to say something about the human condition, about love and hate and sex and desire, you know? So I get the actors and actresses—mainly actresses—and I make the film. Then I contact him and he sells it."

"What about the women Suzy and Poppy saw getting out of the truck?"

He shrugged. "We sometimes used the mill as a setting. There is equipment up there in one of the buildings. Maybe he was making a porn movie. He knows I won't touch porn."

"You won't touch porn..."

"No, oh no. I want to make art? I have always wanted to make art, but no one has ever understood me. Freud said that art gave us access to the deep unconscious, you know. Art is a gateway to truth, ultimate, subjective truth, where the subjective is *transformed* into the objective. *That* is what I want to do."

I stared at the flames dancing in the fireplace and muttered quietly to myself, "Son of a bitch..."

A loud hammering at the door made me start. Isaac stood. I got to my feet and moved around the back of the sofa where I could see the door. The Glock was on the dresser there and I picked it up and checked the magazine. I slipped it in my waistband, under my shirt as Isaac opened the door.

It was Gaynor, with his two remaining men. One of them was Baphomet. The other was the Russian special forces guy with the long, lanky limbs.

Isaac stared at them for a moment. Then stepped back to let them in. "Larry, well, this should be fun. How fucking crazy can things get now, huh?"

Gaynor looked past Isaac and stared straight at me. "Harry Bauer. We have been looking for you. We thought you'd been killed in that accident."

I smiled. "It wasn't an accident, Larry. Where are your other friends? I seem to remember there were seven of you."

They came into the house and Baphomet closed the door. Gaynor walked ahead of the others and entered the living area, taking off his gloves and his coat, which he dumped on the floor.

"I said you were a dangerous man, Harry. But even so I underestimated you. The only thing to do is kill you. Forget about who sent you, and just kill you."

"Not in my house." Isaac was shaking his finger in the negative. "You want to kill him, you take him outside. I don't want blood and DNA all over my furniture and my floor."

Gaynor turned to me and smiled his unpleasant smile. "Well, Harry Bauer, I guess we go for our final walk in the woods."

"Yeah?" I sat on the arm of the sofa. "Suppose you and your two boys come and drag me out?"

His eyes roved over me from head to foot and back again, his smile deepening all the while. "The shape you're in? You're like a walking bruise. And after that tumble you took, I'd be surprised if you didn't have a broken bone or a fractured rib."

"You're not wrong, Gaynor. In this state, maybe even you three could take me. You want to give it a try?" He didn't exactly hesitate, but he didn't leap into action either. I pressed him. "Where are you going to take me? To the same place you took those women? Where are they, by the way?"

I saw Isaac's eyes shift and study Gaynor for a moment. Gaynor shook his head, like he was having trouble coming to a decision. Baphomet and the Russian approached from the door and stood looking at me. Baphomet said, "We gotta kill him, Boss."

I knew what Gaynor was thinking and I laughed, painfully. "What season is it, Crowley?" Baphomet frowned at me. "Yeah, I'm talking to you, Son of the Dark. What season is it? Summer, fall, winter, spring?"

"Spring!" He sounded mad that it was spring.

"So what happens to the snow in spring, Unholy One?"

"Uh...it melts?" The sarcasm was evident in his voice.

"Right, good, now you're thinking! This is a freak snowstorm. In a couple of days it will all start to melt away, revealing what is underneath. And what your genius boss here is thinking is how many God damned bodies are going to show up once it all melts? How many killings can you have in a small town like Balthazar in less than a week, before authorities in high places start to sit up and frown? Isn't that why you intercepted us on the way to Matthias? To give you a chance to clean things up? But you haven't cleaned things up, have you? You've made even more of a mess. It's got way out of hand, hasn't it, Larry?

"Let's see, what have we got? We've got the two girls plus your four boys last night. That makes six, then we've got Hank, who makes seven and four more of your boys tonight, which makes eleven. Kill me and that makes an even dozen. You are going to have the state police crawling all over that mill like ants. Hell, you'll be lucky not to have the Feds here. And where will they be crawling, Larry, besides the mill? You won't be able to rely on Sheriff Walt Davies looking discretely the other way then. He will have to tell everything he knows. And I am wondering, Larry, how much does he know?"

Baphomet and Larry looked at each other for a good five seconds. Then Larry said, "He'll have to go. Do it. Kill him."

EIGHTEEN

GAYNOR LEVELED HIS CANNON AT MY CHEST AND AT the same instant Baphomet and the Russian descended on Isaac and grabbed his skinny arms, one on either side. The dragged him, kicking and screaming toward the door, shouting, "*Larry! Larry, what are you doing? Larry! Tell them to leave me alone!*"

I snarled, "What the hell are you doing?"

He waved the .44 toward the door where they were dragging Isaac out into the snow. "Out!"

Everything slowed right down. I knew I was dead. There was a stillness to the certainty which meant I didn't even question it. The time had come to die. And in that moment of still certainty I saw Isaac's skinny old arms and legs kicking and struggling, and the absolute terror in his eyes as they dragged him, helpless, toward a death he didn't want. A voice in my head said, "There is pain, but the pain is not I."

And I roared, and all the rage and hatred I felt for bastards like Gaynor and Baphomet and the Russian burned in me like a furnace and I leapt across the room. I saw the Redhawk explode and jump in his hand. Pain seared through my chest. But the pain was something apart, that existed in its own right. It was not me. I spun and felt the heat of the slug skim past my face as my heel rammed in a spinning back kick into Gaynor's belly. He reeled back, hit the armchair and fell sprawling on the floor. As I picked up the Redhawk I saw he was spewing foam from his mouth, and I figured he wouldn't be giving me trouble for a while.

I ran, wheezing to the door in time to see the Russian slap Isaac backhanded and knock him down. Baphomet pulled his semi-automatic and pointed it at Isaac, but the Russian said, "No! It makes too much mess. I strangle him." Isaac shrieked, I took aim and blew Baphomet's baphomet right off his head, along with part of his skull and most of his brains.

The recoil from a .44 magnum round is like getting kicked in the hand by a mule with a hornet up its ass, and the pain in my fractured ribs was excruciating. The Russian stood staring a moment at his dead pal, while I tried and failed to breathe. Maybe he was thinking about the mess and how they were going to clean it up.

Then I was hit by a truck from behind. I landed facedown in the snow and lay paralyzed by the spasms in my chest while a fist like a hunk of granite pounded into my ribs. Then there was a shout of rage and as I tried to raise my head the Russian dropped to his knees in front of me, put his two hands on my head and pressed my face down into the snow. I couldn't breathe because the shards of pain in my chest had sent my lungs into spasm, and I couldn't breathe because I had two hundred pounds crushing my face into the snow.

I experienced a moment of resignation. I had known I was going to die, and this was it. This was my moment of death. I had done well to get this far. I heard the snowmobile kick into life and roar away, and knew that Isaac had escaped. I began to convulse and realized I was about to pass out. Then, in a moment of clarity I felt the reassuring weight of the Redhawk still gripped in my right hand, buried and invisible in the snow. I angled it up slightly and pulled the trigger.

There was a violent explosion inches from my face, and then there were screams. Some of them were mine as I dragged in the air. Other's were the Russian's. But I couldn't see where I had hit him. Gaynor had gripped my gun hand with both of his and was trying to lever the muzzle back toward my face. He was screaming hysterically, "*Die! For fucksake die! Die you mother—*"

He didn't get any further. I grabbed the weapon in both hands and yielded enough to his pressure to slam the gun up into his face. He screamed and fell off me, and actually wept, and he rolled about clutching his face. I checked the cylinder and saw I had four rounds left. I wanted Gaynor alive, but I was running out of time. I decided to lock him in the house and reached down to grab him by his collar. He gripped my arm and glared at me. His left eye was blood red, and there was blood streaming down his left cheek.

"Get up," I said. "Be smart and I'll get you a doctor. Do something stupid and I'll kill you stone dead."

He clambered to his feet and, without pausing, smacked me a clumsy elbow in the jaw. I slipped and lost my balance and he scrambled for the remaining snowmobile. I let off one shot, but it went wide and a few seconds later he had vanished into the freezing night, chasing after Isaac.

I got to my feet again, not so much fighting the pain anymore, as the exhaustion which was threatening to overwhelm me. Isaac had gone to get me in a truck adapted to the snow, and that truck had to be in the garage. I staggered inside again and went in search of the kitchen, figuring there would be a door there to the garage. I was right and, as I went through and found the truck and a convertible Jaguar, I was asking myself where the hell Isaac was going, and how Gaynor knew where to follow.

The key was in the ignition and I climbed behind the wheel. There was a remote control on the dash and after I pressed it the big door started to roll back onto the black and white night.

He had headlamps and a row of spots. I turned them all on and rolled out of the garage and onto the road that led to his gate.

The snow was easing and visibility had improved, and with the array of lights, at first, it was easy to follow the tracks Isaac and Gaynor had made, but pretty soon I came to an intersection, and there it was all confusion and chaos. I had to climb, slowly and painfully, down from the cab and hunker down to try and make any sense of the mayhem in the snow. And even then it was hard to make them out.

Eventually I got to my feet and tried to project a map in my mind. My mental map told me that turning left would take me toward town, toward Helen's house. I could see Isaac maybe racing to town to seek protection from the sheriff, but I could not see Gaynor following him there. So I turned right and followed the tracks headed north and a little east into the forest, back toward the damned mill. So maybe he was trying to get back across the border. I doubted he had fuel for that. I glanced at my own gauge and saw it was full.

So he would try to make the mill, switch vehicles there and continue on to St. Stephen. Then all I had to do was block the gate and take him as he came out. I hadn't been going more than a minute when I began to slow. There was a sharp turn to the right up ahead but, through the dense pines, I glimpsed a light. I killed my own lights and slowed to a halt.

The bend was thirty or forty paces away. I thought about moving into the forest to approach from among the trees, but the banks were sheer and slippery with snow and ice. So I proceeded along the road, keeping close to the trees until I reached the bend. Then suddenly I knew where I was, and things started to make sense for the first time.

There was a narrow path through the trees, that came to a clearing with a neat picket fence and lawns that were overgrown at the edges with ferns and saplings. The building itself was large, two floors and an attic, with a gabled roof fringed with bargeboard decorations. There was a small porch and either side of it shuttered windows.

I moved up the path, staying close to the cover of the trees.

The place was silent and still, but I was certain I had seen a light. I moved deeper among the trees and skirted the house, leaving irregular intervals between my steps to minimize the chance of making a noise and alerting anyone to my presence.

Now I saw that at the back of the house stood a church, an old, dilapidated Anglican church, with a spire pointing tall, thin and dark at the black sky, an iron cross perched on top. It had a massive, arched oak door, which stood closed, and four tall, narrow arched windows spaced along the side. This was the old, abandoned vicarage, I told myself, and as I thought that, I saw a glimmer of light in one of those tall, narrow windows.

I thought about it for too long. I was shivering with the cold, everything hurt and my mind was sluggish. But finally I left the cover of the trees and made my way to the big, oak doors. There was an iron ring that served as a handle. I turned it, pushed and pulled, but the door was locked. I stood back, took aim and blew out the lock with a .44 round. That left me two.

The doors slowly swung open. Through them, on the walls, I could see orange candlelight wavering on the walls. But I could see no candles. The pews in the nave were all empty, and over the tall, narrow windows old blankets had been hung.

My first three steps on the stone floor echoed high among the wooden rafters. I stopped at the font. It was dry. And now, through the dense shadows, I could see that the flickering light was coming from behind the altar, and with it I could hear sobbing.

I walked down the aisle and climbed the steps to the great stone slab. The light of the single candle was now bright, wavering in the cold air that was blowing in through the open doors behind me. I moved around the marble slab and looked down. There was a young woman, probably in her early twenties. She was blonde, slim, attractive. On her right cheek she had a purple bruise turning to yellow. She was kneeling on a red cushion with a candle in front of her and gazing up at the wooden crucifix on the wall above her. She didn't look at me. She just prayed, silently moving her mouth, and wept.

I said, "You speak English?"

She closed her eyes and stopped reciting. I could see the candlelight reflected on her wet cheek.

"You come to take us away? Or you come to kill us?"

Her accent was Eastern European. Something told me she was Polish.

"Neither. I'm looking for Larry, Larry Gaynor. Where is he? Where are the other girls?"

She jerked her head at the wall where the crucifix hung. "Behind is priest's office, where he dresses..."

"The vestry."

"They are there." She looked up at me, took in the condition I was in. "Did you break his eye?"

"Yeah."

She nodded and turned back to her prayers.

I left the altar and moved around to the north transept. There I saw another arched, wooden door. I took a hold of the handle and opened it. The sight was not so much surreal as unreal. The room, maybe fifteen foot square, was lit by two candles sitting in a silver candelabra on a heavy wooden table against the wall. In a small fireplace a log fire had burned down to embers.

There were eleven women there, all young, in their early twenties or younger, all attractive and all sitting or standing in a circle on sleeping bags and blankets, staring at me. And in the middle of the floor, lying on his back, shivering badly and whimpering, was Larry. He was sweating profusely and if he didn't get to a doctor soon he was going to die. And it was that thought that made me notice the black-haired woman sitting cross-legged by his left shoulder. She had black eyes too, that were staring hard at me, and in her hands she had an evil-looking letter opener.

I said, "I need him alive."

The black-eyed girl said, "You are police?"

I sighed. "No."

She shrugged. "Elena is making prayer for him soul."

"What's your name?"

"Maria."

"Well it's not his soul I'm worried about, Maria. By tomorrow morning you'll be out of here, picking up the pieces of your life. You can go home, maybe stay in the States, start a new life. But instead you'll be facing murder charges, all of you. Conspiracy to murder. He has done you enough harm; don't let him destroy your lives."

They didn't do or say anything. They just sat there, looking at me.

I ran my fingers through my hair. The exhaustion and the cold were draining the last shreds of energy I had. I spoke, not sure if I was making sense.

"And you have to remember something else, Maria. If you kill him, he's dead and that is the end of it for him. But you, all of you, have to live for the rest of your lives knowing that you have killed another human being. I know what that is like, and believe me, you don't want that."

Maria snorted and looked at me with contempt. "Weak man!"

I scowled at her. "Have you ever killed somebody, Maria?"

"Yes!" She snapped. "Five days ago I put gasoline on a man and make him to burn! Why? Because he is Russian bastard and he is kill my father and my brother and he is rape to my sister. And when I kill him I feel *good!* And this kill, this feeling of kill him is *treasure* for me. I *want* keep it all my life!"

I shook my head, but I had no words for her.

She pointed at the door behind me. "You go! You don't see nothing, you can tell nothing! Go!"

And then, like a macabre ritual they all started to chant it: "Go! Go! Go!"

The door opened behind me and I turned, half stumbling to look. It was Elena, with tears in her eyes. For a moment I thought she was going to beg me to stop them, but she said, quietly, "Go,"

Then all their eyes focused on Gaynor. He was sobbing and

trembling. Maria raised the jeweled letter opener above her head in both hands, sheer, evil hatred transfigured her face and she drove the blade down with a shrill scream. It plunged into his chest and his feet lifted off the floor and kicked in a strangely childlike motion. His body jerked and twitched for a few seconds, and then it was over.

NINETEEN

I TOOK A HANDKERCHIEF FROM MY POCKET, WIPED THE prints off the handle of the letter opener and then gripped it in my hand. After a moment I said, "There was a fight. You were scared and you were hiding, looking away. You don't remember any details. Only that Larry and I had a fight. OK?" They all nodded. "OK, we are going home."

They didn't move. Instead they collectively put their heads in their hands and started to cry. I left them to it and walked the fifty yards to the truck, fired it up and drove it to the vicarage. Somehow I got them all in, four up front and eight in back, sitting on each other's laps and cramped on the floor, all wrapped in their blankets and sleeping bags, and we headed back toward town. The progress was slow and painful. We were all freezing and, cramped as they were, each bump and lurch brought choruses of cries and shouts of pain.

Eventually we came to the intersection where I had been a little earlier. Left led to Isaac's house, and right led to town. I turned right and kept going. The snow had eased off and finally stopped, and overhead the clouds were not so heavy, not bellying so low. And then we came to a turn up ahead, where I saw a glow of light wash the trees and the snow. I reached for the Redhawk, with its two rounds left, but my head was telling me, unbelievable as it might seem, Isaac had got to the sheriff, and they had come to look for me.

I honked the horn and flashed the lights to let them know we were coming, and some of the girls started to shout and cry out. And when we rounded the bend we found two trucks sitting in the middle of the road with their headlamps glaring at us. I shielded my eyes and Sheriff Walt Davies' voice bellowed out over his bullhorn.

"*Stop the vehicle! Climb down from the vehicle and keep your hands in the air!*"

I swore violently under my breath and said to the girls, "You stay here. Don't get down."

I stuck both my hands out of the window, then opened the door and stepped out into the snow. Shielding my eyes, I shouted, "Sheriff! I have twelve women in the truck! They are sick and in serious need of medical help! They are not getting out of the vehicle. Some of them are barefoot!"

His voice came back, bellowing over the bullhorn, "*What the hell...!*" Then it crackled and the man himself appeared, trudging through the snow toward me.

"That you, Bauer? What the hell! We found the truck abandoned! You know how much that truck cost? Where the hell have you been?"

"Shut up, Walt! I'll explain everything over hot coffee and a bottle of whiskey. Meantime, did Isaac Boothe show up and tell you where I was?"

He shook his head. "No." Then he marched past me and poked his head in the truck. "Holy sweet Jesus!" he said, then turned back to his trucks. "Dip them damned lights, will ya!" The lights dipped and he went on. "You, Deputy Smith. You take this bus and drive it back to the office. You get Doc Johansen out of his bed and make sure he tends to these women. They'll need food and drink too."

"First get them somewhere warm, Sheriff, where the doctor

can see them. We'll call at Helen's on the way and get her making hot food and drink at the restaurant."

He nodded, the deputy climbed aboard and the truck roared off toward town, accompanied by screams and howls of pain and complaints about the speed.

We climbed into his truck and he turned it around, headed back for town and Helen's house, followed by the big RAM we had driven that morning. As he did it he asked me, "So, what the hell happened to you?"

I spoke automatically, but my mind was split in two. One part was trying not to think about all the different kinds of pain I was experiencing, while the other tried to make sense of what had happened.

"We were ambushed," I said, and then, "So Isaac didn't show?"

"No, why should he?" I stared at his face a moment, thinking of all the things he didn't know. "So, why are you out here?"

"I told you we found your truck abandoned. The weather's clearing and we finally got the phone lines back. Called Machias and they said you hadn't showed up—that's when we went looking for you and found the truck—so we figured we'd better go up to the mill like you said. Machias said they'd be sending some people up, and to radio from the mill if things got ugly."

I smiled to myself. "Things got pretty ugly."

"Wait, you was ambushed? Who ambushed you?"

"Isaac's partner, Larry Gaynor. He sells his porn movies for him."

"Oh, geez!"

"So, if he didn't go to you, where the hell did he go?"

My brain was aching and the sheriff kept interrupting my thinking. Now he was saying, "Now, wait a minute. So who are these women? Where'd they come from?"

I went to answer but my jaw hung loose. Suddenly my mind was racing. I turned and stared at him. "They're not porn actresses."

"Yeah, I can see that. Who are they?"

I was still talking like an automaton, staring at his face. "One of them is called Elena, she's Polish and probably a Catholic, another is Maria, and she is from Ukraine—*Jesus Christ!*"

"What?"

"*How could I be so stupid!*"

We had arrived at Helen's house. I turned to Walt and grabbed a fistful of his jacket.

"Walt, listen to me. Go get Helen. Take her to the restaurant and feed those girls."

"Where the hell are you going?"

"To Rosie Jones' house. Go!" I jumped down and ran, shouting over my shoulder, "Then come and get me!"

It wasn't far from Helen's place, set back from the road behind an evergreen hedge and surrounded by the tall, dark silhouettes of poplar trees. I pushed through the gate and stood, looking. A path had been cleared to the front door, but a single set of footprints were still visible. I followed them, careful not to tread on them, and came to the door. I didn't press the bell or knock. The door was already open—just a few inches—and there was snow on the mat inside. I listened, but heard nothing. So I pushed the door open and stepped inside.

The hall was still and silent. There was light coming from somewhere but it was hard to tell from where. I could make out a rush mat on the floor laid over what looked like a Persian carpet underneath. There was a coat stand on my right beside a mahogany dresser with an oval mirror. There were prints on the walls of hunting scenes.

The hall formed a dogleg at the end, where it turned to the right, with double doors straight ahead and another door on the left. I took three silent strides and saw that the corridor led down to a flight of stairs on the right, and described another dogleg to the left, possibly to the kitchen. The light was filtering down from the upper floor.

I stopped to listen again. Again I heard nothing but the stillness of the house.

The door on my left gave onto a large closet that housed brooms and mops and a vacuum cleaner, and smelt of furniture wax. I closed it and opened the double doors which gave onto a large drawing room. The drapes on the far side were open, displaying large sliding glass doors onto a backyard. Dim, blue snow light filtered in, making inky silhouettes of a sofa, armchairs, a tall lamp in the corner.

For a moment I thought I saw a large dog lying on the carpet in front of a cold fireplace, but I could hear no breathing and the shape looked somehow wrong. I moved into the room and approached the dark form.

It was a body, a large body, and it was motionless. I hunkered down and now, close up, I recognized Mongo. I felt for his pulse, but the cold, waxy texture of his skin told me he was dead.

I stood and went back to the hall. After a moment I called out, "Isaac?" There was no reply so I called a little louder, "Rosie?"

The reply, when it came, was barely audible, like it was suppressed by terror.

"*Harry...?*" and then, "*Harry, I'm upstairs.*"

I frowned hard. It was Rosie's voice. I thought about Mongo lying dead on the living room floor. I thought about the single set of tracks leading from the gate to the door. My belly was burning with a strange fear. I moved toward the stairs.

"Rosie, is Isaac there with you?"

Her voice was barely a whisper, a whisper that seemed to filter through the air, "*Upstairs...*"

I climbed the stairs to the landing. A single bulb in a globe gave a stark light. There were several doors, but one stood open ajar. The room within was dark.

"Rosie? Miss Jones?"

Again the stage whisper, "*In the bedroom...*"

"Is Isaac with you?"

There was only silence.

After a moment I crossed the landing, placed my fingertips on the door and pushed.

I felt a sudden nausea in my stomach. My skin went cold and prickled. Rosie was not there. Isaac was. I recognized him, partly illuminated by the limpid blue light leaning in through the window. He was sitting in a rocking chair staring at me. He had no expression on his face.

"Isaac?"

She spoke without inflection, like an automaton, but very quietly, "Go away."

"What's going on, Isaac?"

"Go away. Get out of here."

Then I saw her. I saw her reflection in the dark glass of the window. I could see the luminous oblong of the bedroom door leading to the landing behind me. And I could see her shape, silhouetted black in the light. She was standing very still.

I said, "You killed Mongo."

Nobody answered. I said:

"And the girls."

The voice from behind me, still just a whisper, said, "*Mongo...*"

"Mongo killed the girls. It had never occurred to me until a few minutes ago. What does a lady like you, living in a town like Balthazar, need with a bodyguard like Mongo?"

I saw her silhouette shift in the glass. She had moved a little closer, but she didn't speak.

"But of course, if you were dealing with Gaynor, that was a whole different ball game. Then you would need protection. And all along I had assumed it was Isaac who was dealing with Gaynor. Isaac with the bad behavior, Isaac with the bad reputation for drugs and sex, Isaac who was making the dirty movies. And of course he was dealing with Gaynor, weren't you, Isaac?" He was as silent as Rosie. I didn't wait for an answer. "But every time I talked to you I was struck by the same thing, the same thing that always made me uncomfortable. You were sincere. You're as crazy as a box of frogs, but you're sincere. You really believe all that shit about altered consciousness and erotism. You actually disapprove of pornography."

His voice was barely a flutter. "I would never approve of the exploitation of women. Of anyone..."

"I should have seen it from the start. Isaac always was, and always will be, an idealist. He lost his shot at fame and fortune because of it. But I didn't see it until it was too late."

Her reflected shadow drew a little closer. I kept talking.

"Even when I saw the girls in your church, I didn't register completely."

There was a soft laugh. "You wouldn't expect it of me, would you?"

"No. But of course, the sawmill was yours. It was the Jones sawmill, founded by your ancestors. It didn't dawn on me until I saw the girls at the church. The vicarage, the church, the mill, the March Mom March, Emily Jones. I had partly registered it, but what hadn't struck me was, if the sawmill was yours, you must have sold it to Larry Gaynor. And once I had realized that," I turned my head so I was talking over my shoulder, "whichever way you looked at it, it didn't square up with Isaac being behind the killing of Suzy and Polly."

"No..."

"If Isaac introduced you to Larry Gaynor, it meant you sold the mill to a man you knew was involved in pornography and who knows what else. And that was not how you put yourself across. But if Isaac didn't introduce you, that meant you were the one who found Gaynor, sold him the mill on the condition he changed the name, and introduced him to Isaac. And that made sense." I turned half a step to my right. "Because then there would be nothing to connect Gaynor's business to you, and everything to connect it to Isaac. And that was when I remembered that it was you who first suggested Isaac to me as the girls' killer. You were framing him from the start."

She barked a single laugh. It was startling in the silence. "And why wouldn't I, after all he has cost me, after all he has taken from me. He robbed my whole life. I *believed* in him! I had a brilliant career ahead of me as a professor at Harvard! I was an outstanding anthropologist. I loved my subject! I was writing a book. It would have made my name."

"And then Isaac came along."

I waited. Inched a little farther around to see her.

"We have always been here, the Jones. We created this town. Balthazar Jones. Four hundred years. Before America even existed as a nation. We have been doctors, lawyers, vicars, and I was going to publish a standard work on social psychology and anthropology." She went silent for a moment. When she spoke again her voice was like distilled poison. "And then Isaac came along. The upstart, Johnny come lately, Isaac *Boothe!* Brilliant, genius, rising star of Freudian psychoanalysis and neurology."

"And you fell in love with him."

"I defied my family for him. I defied the college for him. I defied the whole *fucking world* for him. I experimented with drugs, did unspeakable things in the name of expanding consciousness...for him."

She took another step closer. Her face, already in shadow, grew darker.

"I believed it would all be worth it. I believed he was going to be somebody. I believed we were both going to rise together to be something, to leave our mark on history, transform society. The whole counterculture was the tide on which we would be carried to greatness.

"Instead, they fired him. And he took it like the peasant farmer he is. He didn't fight, he didn't use it to expose Harvard for the establishment tool it was. He just took it and scuttled away, like a cringing rat, hid in his little shithole of a house and made pornographic shit! And left me to rot! Abandoned me! *Betrayed me!* They kicked me out because of him, but they didn't pay me off. Oh, no! I wasn't a brilliant genius like him! No payoff for me!"

She took another step closer. She was less than three feet from me now.

"But we Jones don't take things lying down. We *fight!* And I fought back! I survived. *I* became a very rich woman! A very *powerful woman!*"

"Powerful enough," I said quietly, "to have two young women killed."

Her voice was like the slow rasp of sandpaper. "I can have anyone killed. I can kill. I own this town. I own these people. I can have them all killed. I killed Mongo with my own hands. I killed Isaac with my own hands."

"Why, Rosie? Why did you kill them? It's not because they discovered you were making movies, was it? Because you don't make movies, do you, Rosie?"

"Larry makes movies."

"Larry makes movies, but you don't. You traffic girls, don't you, Rosie. You sell girls. You sell girls for the Russian Mafia. They send them over from Poland to Larry in Canada, and you bring them into the States."

There was a smile in her voice. "And you would not *believe* how much money you can make buying and selling people."

"But it's over, Rosie. We found the girls, Gaynor is dead..."

"It ain't over till the fat broad sings, buster. There are plenty more Larrys where that one came from. Now, here is how we are going to do this, Harry. Isaac is nearly dead. He is bleeding out slowly from a nasty cut in his belly, and you both need to accept that you are going to die tonight, in the next while. There is no way back. Death is here with us, among us. The choice you have is this: to die fast and relatively painlessly. Or to die slowly, in lots of pain."

She waited. I frowned. Isaac sobbed, "Kill her for fuck's sake, Harry! What are you waiting for?"

She pointed at the bed. "Take your clothes off and get in the bed."

I looked at the bed, then back at her. My breathing was loud in my ears. Isaac half screamed, "*Kill her, Harry! Just kill her!*"

Suddenly she brushed past me. Too late I saw the glint of steel in her hand. She grabbed Isaac's face and pulled it back over the headrest of the chair, exposing his throat. He started to sob.

The light from the landing washed her face. It was hard, and her eyes were small and dark.

"OK, Bauer. Hesitate another second and I give him a Colombian necktie."

"No! Rosie, wait!"

I took a step forward, holding out my hand. She went on, "You know what that is? I cut his throat under his chin, I pull out his tongue through the cut and I slice it off. It is no more than the bastard deserves. That's how we begin. It only gets worse after that."

Isaac had started crying like a child, moaning and sobbing. His voice was shrill. "*What the fuck is wrong with you, Harry? Kill her!*"

"I have been told that bleeding out, if the blade is extremely sharp, can be a beautiful, peaceful experience. Like freezing to death. Unfortunately, this blade has already had some use tonight, and I may have to do some sawing and hacking. So, why don't you just take your clothes off, Harry, and get on the bed?"

I shook my head. "No, wait, listen to me."

She wasn't listening. She was laughing. "You will be humiliated and discredited as you deserve. You will die as lovers—jealous passion? Suicide pact? Who knows? You will kill each other, in each other's arms." She threw back her head and screamed with laughter.

I looked at Isaac. He was crying in great moaning sobs. I knew I wouldn't be able to put him through the nightmare of torture she was describing. I said, "I'm sorry," and pulled off my jacket.

The actions were contradictory. I was doing what she was telling me to do, but at the same time I was apologizing, saying I wasn't going to do it. For a couple of seconds she was confused, paralyzed, and a couple of seconds was all I was going to get. I stepped up and shoved my jacket in her face with my right hand and with my left I grabbed her wrist and wrenched it back. She was weak and frail, but she fought savagely, frenziedly trying to bend the blade around to get at Isaac's throat. She thrashed and kicked and I pulled her away from the chair, shouting at her to be still. Her feet stumbled, caught in the jacket that had dropped at her feet, and she fell.

Next thing she was scrambling to her feet and running. I went after her. She clattered down the stairs, and by the time I got to the bottom she had burst out the door and was running down the dark, freezing path. Down the road I saw two sets of headlamps approaching at speed. Rosie hesitated a moment, shielded her eyes, looked back at me and then, taking the handle of the knife in both hands, she placed the blade against her belly, went down on her knees and fell forward into the snow. She gave a cry and a gasp, and fell silent.

EPILOGUE

Isaac was lying in the hospital bed. He was hooked up to a series of monitors but he had color in his cheeks and he looked OK. As usual he was leering.

"In the good old days," he was saying, "nurses had to wear proper uniforms, with aprons and bonnets. How is a man supposed to recover when all the nurses dress the same in baggy pants and coats?"

Helen laughed. "I told you not to vote Democrat! See?"

I smiled. "When are you going home?"

"They figure another week. Don't know what I'm going to do. Harvard has cut me off and I've lost my business." He shrugged and sighed, but pretty soon the leer was back. "Tell you the truth, I was getting pretty bored with the movies. There are only so many erotic things you can do before it starts getting repetitive." He grinned at Helen. "Know what I mean?"

She arched a severe eyebrow at him. "No, Isaac, I do not!"

"Well, take it from me. So I've written to an agent in New York. Told them to contact Harper Collins and offer them my story. It's got everything, controversy, defiance, lots of sex and now, thanks to you, violence too! I told them a two million dollar advance would be about right. Then there's Hollywood. I see

Chris Pratt as the young genius Isaac Boothe, and maybe Hugh Jackman as the older, wiser man telling his tale. I'm going to call it, *The Tao of the Power of Flowers*."

"It has to be a smash hit."

"Hey, who's a genius round here?"

We left him making lewd remarks to his surgeon about how he'd like to see her in surgical gloves, and made our way down to the parking lot, where my Chimera was waiting. When we got there, Helen sat on the hood and stared at me.

"What?" I asked her.

"What are you going to do now?"

I shrugged. "I thought we could go for dinner."

"Dinner?" she looked at her watch. "It's just eleven AM."

"Not here," I said, "in San Francisco. I haven't had my holiday yet. It's only about two and a half thousand miles, and on the way we could pass through Wyoming and you could show me how to be a real man."

She smiled. "Oh, I would *love* to do that," she said.

Don't miss SIMPLE KILL. The riveting sequel in the Harry Bauer Thriller series.

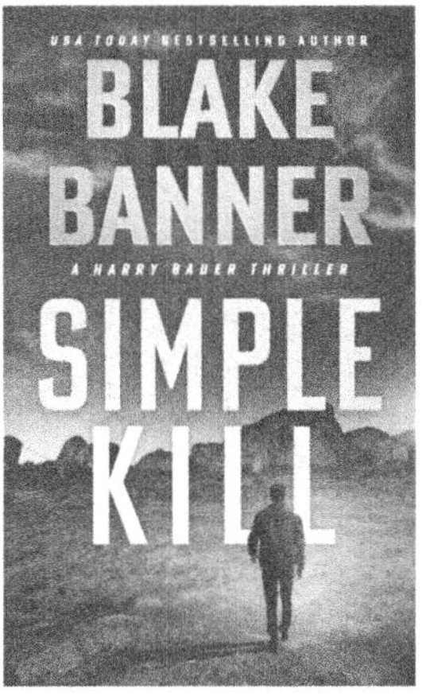

Scan the QR code below to purchase SIMPLE KILL.

Or go to: righthouse.com/simple-kill

NOTE: flip to the very end to read an exclusive sneak peak...

DON'T MISS ANYTHING!

If you want to stay up to date on all new releases in this series, with this author, or with any of our new deals, you can do so by joining our newsletters below.

In addition, you will immediately gain access to our entire *Right House VIP Library,* which includes many riveting Mystery and Thriller novels for your enjoyment!

righthouse.com/email

(Easy to unsubscribe. No spam. Ever.)

ALSO BY BLAKE BANNER

Up to date books can be found at:
www.righthouse.com/blake-banner

ROGUE THRILLERS

Gates of Hell (Book 1)
Hell's Fury (Book 2)

ALEX MASON THRILLERS

Odin (Book 1)
Ice Cold Spy (Book 2)
Mason's Law (Book 3)
Assets and Liabilities (Book 4)
Russian Roulette (Book 5)
Executive Order (Book 6)
Dead Man Talking (Book 7)
All The King's Men (Book 8)
Flashpoint (Book 9)
Brotherhood of the Goat (Book 10)
Dead Hot (Book 11)
Blood on Megiddo (Book 12)
Son of Hell (Book 13)

HARRY BAUER THRILLER SERIES

Dead of Night (Book 1)
Dying Breath (Book 2)
The Einstaat Brief (Book 3)
Quantum Kill (Book 4)
Immortal Hate (Book 5)
The Silent Blade (Book 6)
LA: Wild Justice (Book 7)

Breath of Hell (Book 8)
Invisible Evil (Book 9)
The Shadow of Ukupacha (Book 10)
Sweet Razor Cut (Book 11)
Blood of the Innocent (Book 12)
Blood on Balthazar (Book 13)
Simple Kill (Book 14)
Riding The Devil (Book 15)
The Unavenged (Book 16)
The Devil's Vengeance (Book 17)
Bloody Retribution (Book 18)
Rogue Kill (Book 19)
Blood for Blood (Book 20)

DEAD COLD MYSTERY SERIES

An Ace and a Pair (Book 1)
Two Bare Arms (Book 2)
Garden of the Damned (Book 3)
Let Us Prey (Book 4)
The Sins of the Father (Book 5)
Strange and Sinister Path (Book 6)
The Heart to Kill (Book 7)
Unnatural Murder (Book 8)
Fire from Heaven (Book 9)
To Kill Upon A Kiss (Book 10)
Murder Most Scottish (Book 11)
The Butcher of Whitechapel (Book 12)
Little Dead Riding Hood (Book 13)
Trick or Treat (Book 14)
Blood Into Wine (Book 15)
Jack In The Box (Book 16)
The Fall Moon (Book 17)
Blood In Babylon (Book 18)
Death In Dexter (Book 19)
Mustang Sally (Book 20)

A Christmas Killing (Book 21)
Mommy's Little Killer (Book 22)
Bleed Out (Book 23)
Dead and Buried (Book 24)
In Hot Blood (Book 25)
Fallen Angels (Book 26)
Knife Edge (Book 27)
Along Came A Spider (Book 28)
Cold Blood (Book 29)
Curtain Call (Book 30)

THE OMEGA SERIES

Dawn of the Hunter (Book 1)
Double Edged Blade (Book 2)
The Storm (Book 3)
The Hand of War (Book 4)
A Harvest of Blood (Book 5)
To Rule in Hell (Book 6)
Kill: One (Book 7)
Powder Burn (Book 8)
Kill: Two (Book 9)
Unleashed (Book 10)
The Omicron Kill (Book 11)
9mm Justice (Book 12)
Kill: Four (Book 13)
Death In Freedom (Book 14)
Endgame (Book 15)

ABOUT US

Right House is an independent publisher created by authors for readers. We specialize in Action, Thriller, Mystery, and Crime novels.

If you enjoyed this novel, then there is a good chance you will like what else we have to offer! Please stay up to date by using any of the links below.

Join our mailing lists to stay up to date --> righthouse.com/email
Visit our website --> righthouse.com
Contact us --> contact@righthouse.com

facebook.com/righthousebooks
x.com/righthousebooks
instagram.com/righthousebooks

EXCLUSIVE SNEAK PEAK OF...

SIMPLE KILL

CHAPTER 1

I PARKED IN THE SHADE OF A SPINDLY OAK TREE NEAR the corner of East 35th and 3rd Avenue and sat for a moment looking at the green awning over the entrance to the fourteen-storey apartment block at number 166.

Jane, the colonel, had come to see me at home, in my brownstone on James Baldwin Place. The colonel was Cobra's woman in the CIA. Cobra knew she was with the Company, but the very top brass at the Company knew she was with Cobra. The last time we had met it had not been real friendly, so I was surprised to see her at my front door. In theory she was Head of Operations. In practice I always dealt with the brigadier. He'd been my commanding officer in the SAS and we understood each other. Besides, the colonel and I just didn't seem to work.

But there she was, sitting in my living room, in her navy blue suit and her nice legs, telling me that Jan van Hoek had to die. He was a very bad man. He was a mercenary and, in the last five years alone, he had organized and executed the massacre of over three thousand people—men, women, children, the elderly and sick—in three villages in the Republic of Cabinda-Itumba, on the west coast of Africa. He had even received a medal from President Cosmo Manuel for his bravery in participating personally in the massacres. Now he was in New York, in his apartment on the fourteenth floor of 166 East 35th Street. And he was alone. *Get in your car and go and kill him.*

I climbed out of my ancient Golf GTI and crossed the road. Jan van Hoek had been a mercenary for over twenty years. Even in his late forties he would be dangerous, but he would not be expecting me. It would be simple, straightforward.

I crossed the cool, dark marble lobby to the elevators and rode one of them to the fourteenth floor. I stepped out into the air-conditioned corridor, carpeted in red with pictures of vases of flowers on the walls, and walked to the last door on the right. His was the corner apartment.

The door was opened after about thirty seconds by a man in jeans and a vest who was talking over his shoulder while he chewed something. His chewing slowed as he looked at my eyes. When you've been in the business that long, you recognize a fellow killer. You smell them and your hackles rise.

"Yeah?"

"I think I have the wrong address."

He shook his head. "It's OK, she's leaving. Come on in."

Maybe I should have turned around and walked away, left it to somebody else. But something was wrong and I wanted to know what it was. I followed him inside, through a small entrance hall to a large living room-dining room with a large corner terrace beyond sliding glass doors.

The furnishings were minimalist, on bare parquet floors, and in a white, leather armchair there was a woman sitting staring at me. She had very black hair tied in a knot at the back of her neck and very dark eyes that watched me carefully as I came in. She had a small plastic bottle of water in her hand. It was almost empty. She took a swig, still watching me, and set it on the coffee table. Van Hoek said, "Adelina, can we finish this later? Let's eat tonight. I'll call you."

She sighed like she was losing patience with something and stood. She gave me another look—this one would have killed if it could have—and made her way into the hall, followed by Jan. On an impulse I pulled out my handkerchief, picked up the bottle and put it in my pocket. There was some harsh whispering and after a moment I heard the door close. A few seconds later Jan van Hoek stepped back into the living room and grinned.

"Hi, who did you say you were?" The accent was Dutch, maybe South African.

"I didn't. Are you Jan van Hoek?"

"Sure, what's it about?"

I'd brought the Maxim 9. Unlike a Sig with a suppressor attached, the Maxim fits into a holster under your arm. Perhaps I should have killed him there and then, according to instructions, but I'd been seen—and scrutinized—by an unknown woman, and when he was dead she was going to tell the cops I was the last person to see Jan alive. I didn't relish that idea.

I pulled the Maxim and showed it to him. "We're going to go for a ride. I don't want to kill you, Jan, we just need to talk about a few things. Provided we can reach an understanding, you go back to your life and you never hear from me again. Give me trouble and I'll shoot you stone dead right in the lobby or on the sidewalk. This is New York, Jan, nobody gives a damn and nobody wants to get involved."

"Who sent you?"

"Quit stalling, Jan. I'll tell you when we get where we're going. Meantime get your jacket, and make sure to bring your wallet, your driver's license and your phone." After a moment I asked him, "Do you smoke?"

He'd gone into the bedroom, but he leaned out of the door to frown at me.

"Yeah, why?"

"Bring your cigarettes and your lighter too."

When he emerged from the bedroom he was looking at me curiously. He was wondering why I'd allowed him to be alone in his bedroom, getting his jacket. He had obviously slipped his shoulder holster on with a semi-automatic under his arm, and he was wondering why I had allowed him to do that.

That was fine by me, because a man who has been abducted for the purpose of execution does not normally bring along his cigarettes and lighter, his billfold, his driver's license and his Glock 17. It wouldn't get me off the hook if Adelina fingered me, but it would put a big question mark in any investigator's mind.

I said, "We'll take your car."

"Yeah, sure, no problem." He gave something that would have liked to be a smile, but lacked any real will.

We took the elevator all the way down to the bowels of the building. I followed him through a spring-loaded door into the parking garage. It was dark and smelled of dirt, oil and carbon monoxide. He led me to a Mercedes convertible SL 63 Roadster and I told him, "Get behind the wheel." He did as I said and I got in beside him. "The Bronx, Soundview Park. Leave the car on O'Brien Avenue. You know where it is?"

"Clason Point, near the amphitheater."

"Let's go."

The tires screamed in the shadows as we spiraled toward the road. Once we were out in the sun, headed north on the FDR, he said, "Be straight with me. You gonna kill me?" He glanced at me, then back at the road.

"I told you that's not what this is about."

He was silent then till we'd crossed the eastern Boulevard Bridge and peeled off onto Bruckner Boulevard. Then he said, "So what *is* it about? Do you have to keep me in suspense like this?"

There was a tremor in his voice and I could see he was gripping the wheel tight. I smiled. "What makes you so sure it's an execution?"

"Hell!" He gestured at the Maxim in my lap. "A guy turns up at your house with a suppressed semi-automatic under his arm and says, 'We're going for a ride.' What are you going to think?" He glanced at me. "I mean, it's not a Glock or a Sig Sauer, like any normal person would carry. It's a fucking Maxim 9. They are designed for executions, man!"

I watched him for a while, asking myself why the hell I should make the bastard feel better. He turned into the broad expanse of Soundview Avenue, with its low, flat buildings painted gaudy yellow, dirty white and sickly gray, its steel tubing and chicken-wire fences and concrete yards.

"Who was the woman?"

He glanced at me. "What?"

I gave a small laugh and shook my head. "Why are you asking me 'What?' Jan. You heard the question. Who is she?"

He didn't answer. I said:

"You want me to shoot you in the knee? I can do it now or when we get to the park. I don't mind. I don't want this to get ugly, Jan. I want it to be simple, no blood, no pain, no screaming and weeping. But you start bullshitting me and things start to get very ugly very quickly. Don't do it."

He'd been shaking his head throughout. Now he said, "No, no, no... It's OK, I didn't mean... It's fine, it's fine."

"Who is she?"

"Oh, man," because of the accent he made it sound like *Oh, men,* but he meant *Oh, man.* "You put me in such a difficult situation—"

"We're not friends, Jan. Don't get intimate with me. We're not going to get drunk together and swap war stories. This is the third time I'm asking you and it will be the last. Who is she?"

He accelerated down Soundview and turned right at Patterson. There he took a deep breath, turned left into Beach Avenue and at the end, where it becomes a dirt track and they called it O'Brien Avenue, he stopped and killed the engine. For a moment he sat with his lower lip gripped between his teeth. Finally he said, quietly, "She's my daughter. She's the only good thing I ever did in my life. Please, please don't hurt her."

I searched his face for the tell. I didn't see it, but I said, "Bullshit. I've studied your file, Jan. You don't have any kids."

"Of course I don't!" He rolled his eyes. "Not on paper! That's all a bloke like me needs, people knowing he has a daughter. She'd never stand a chance!" He stared at me for a moment, his face tight and his eyebrows high on his forehead. "She's illegitimate, a bastard."

"Who's her mother?"

"Mariana dos Santos, a Portuguese doctor. Most beautiful woman I had ever seen. She was everything I wasn't. I was twenty, she must have been thirty-something. We moved into the village with the Land Rovers and the guns, y'know? We knew the men were working for the Demos."

"Demos?"

"Cabinda-Itumba Democratic Liberation Front. CIDLF. Not a great acronym, but the red bastards rallied to it. She was there with the *Médecins Sans Frontières*. She was brave." He nodded several times, gazing out at the tangle of wild trees in the park. He grinned at me, looking along his eyes. "She came at me with a scalpel, boy. We had thirty men in Land Rovers armed with assault rifles, rounding everybody up into the main square, and she comes at me like a fucking wildcat, holding a scalpel. I'll tell you, I fell in love with her right there on the spot. I grabbed her, disarmed her, carried her into the hospital hut and took her right there. The one time, and she got pregnant. It was meant to be. God, the Universe, the Devil, whatever. It was meant."

"You raped her."

He shook his head, dismissed the notion out of hand. "Nah! She wanted it. Woman like that? What normal woman goes to fucking Cabinda-Itumba, in the middle of the jungle to work as a doctor? She was there looking for adventure. It was primal. We were meant to be together for those minutes. Man and woman in the jungle, making life, surrounded by fucking death."

"So you killed everyone in the village except her."

"I had a sergeant drive her back to Buco, and from there she was sent to the capital city of Cabinda."

"And back to Portugal?"

He became serious and shook his head. "Nah. Government held her there, in Cabinda. They said the child had been conceived in Cabinda-Itumba and should be born there."

"You pulled strings so she wouldn't leave."

He didn't answer. "When the child was born they told her she could leave, but the child had to stay and be raised as Cabindalese. So she stayed with her baby, for five years, but when the child was five years old, Mariana died. Dr. Mariana dos Santos. *Médecins Sans Frontières*. Heroine. Dead."

"You had her killed."

"Of course not! Why would I do that? I told her if she married me, recognized me as her husband and the father of her child, we could leave, make a life in Europe, the States, wherever she liked." He looked me in the eye. "You know what the ungrateful bitch did? She spat in my face. In the end I think she died of depression, trapped like a rat in that shithole."

"This was the woman you were in love with."

He glanced at me and there was insolence in his eyes. "Fuck you."

"Get out of the car."

He didn't do it straight away. He gave my face a once-over first. Maybe he was trying to work out whether I was going to kill him; maybe he was wondering if he could take me right there and then. The Maxim answered at least one of those questions and he climbed out of the car while I got out the other side.

There was a low, dilapidated wire fence separating the dirt track from the park. It was easy to step over and we moved in among the wild ferns, grass and saplings that made of the park something between a savannah and a jungle. We trudged across the two hundred yards of scrub that separated us from a fringe of woodland that framed the park along the mouth of the Bronx River. When we came to the footpath he stopped and looked at me. Something in his eyes told me he had decided I was going to kill him. I said, "Relax, will you? Down to the water's edge. The water interferes with listening devices. I'm being careful."

A spasm of irritation contracted his face. "What the fuck is this about?"

"Quit stalling and I'll tell you. Let's go, down to the water."

We picked our way through the trees to the big rocks that flanked the river. I moved down, close to the water edge, and pointed to a rock about six feet from me.

"Sit down." As he sat I said, "Before I tell you what this is about, I need you to confirm a couple of things for me."

"Like what?"

"Tell me about Tanda Matiaba, Caio and Chimbete."

His eyebrows shot up and his mouth sagged open in a smile. He gave a small laugh. "You're kidding me. What are you, Interpol or some shit?"

I smiled. "More like some shit. There are certain things a Western democratic government cannot be seen to do. We take care of those things while providing credible deniability to respectable governments. Remember Roosevelt? Speak softly but carry a big stick? We are the big stick, but we can't be seen to be."

To my surprise he laughed and said, "Son of a gun...you're recruiting me! I don't believe it! You're fucking recruiting me to do your fucking dirty work!" He threw back his head and laughed out loud. I continued to smile, but said nothing. If this made it easier, so be it. When he was done he nodded slowly three times, watching me.

"OK," he said, "I'll tell you about Tanda Matiaba, Caio and Chimbete, but let me warn you, a guy like me does not come cheap."

"Don't worry," I said. "Nobody pays higher rates than us."

CHAPTER 2

He reached in his pocket and pulled out a pack of Camels. He shook one free and took it into his mouth straight from the pack, then lit up with an old, brass Zippo. He took a deep breath and blew out a long stream of smoke.

"You know." He said it as a statement, then glanced at me as though for confirmation. "Just because they changed the regime and pulled down the wall, didn't mean the Cold War was over. Right? The Cold War was never about Communism, or freedom. Like the Eagles said, freedom, that's just some people talking. It was about power. It was always about power. You know that."

He took a drag and looked out at where the black water from the Bronx flowed into the East River.

"Must be all of five years ago now. Russia was pushing its influence in Africa. You guys always thought of yourselves as the heirs to the British Empire, never mind the War of Independence. What's a little Oedipal in-fighting among empires? Keep it in the family. No problem. So as the British Empire faded, America stepped in to mop up Africa with a few trade concessions here and a few exclusive exploitation contracts there. And why not? We gave them hospitals, railways and fucking schools, why shouldn't we make something on the deal?"

He looked like he wanted an answer so I said, "Keep talking."

"But all these little upstart republics keep discovering fuckin' socialism and communism. And you know what? When all you've ever known is tribal kingdoms and the British Empire, socialism and communism make a lot more sense than bloody democracy. I mean, I'm President Cosmo Manuel of Cabinda-Itumba and you make me an offer, 'You can either have a multi-party system where the leader gets changed every four or five years, and the people get to vote and have guaranteed liberties, or you can have absolute power for life and the people shut up and do as they're told. Which do *you* think I'm going to go for?"

"So Russian-backed socialism was spreading in Africa. So what?"

"So the CIA sent a delegation to visit President Cosmo Manuel and told him, 'You guarantee our interests in Cabinda-Itumba, crush any filthy communist-backed movements, and we will make you a very rich, powerful man and put Cabinda-Itumba on the world stage."

"You know this or are you just speculating conspiracy theories?"

He gave me a small laugh and a pitying smile. "I was at the fucking meeting, mate. I saw the whole thing. I even recorded it. I've got the recordings at my apartment, on my fucking laptop."

He flicked ash using his ring finger and stared down between his feet.

"So the president promised the CIA men he would stamp out Russian-backed movements forever in Cabinda-Itumba. And he sent me and my boys of the Praetorian Guard to defend freedom and equality, and the sacred values of democracy, by annihilating the three main villages which were known to give succor to the communist rebels. We had experience doing that kind of thing. It wasn't the first village we'd exterminated over the years. So we got in the Land Rovers, we drove to the villages, tortured the townsfolk until they told us where the boys were, the rebels, and then we systematically killed everybody. It was pretty heavy, even for us. Couple of the lads were sick."

He looked at me suddenly, like he'd had a sudden thought. "You ever done extermination work?" I shook my head. "They tell you it gets easier. It doesn't. It gets harder every time you do it. And it stays with you." He poked at his head with his finger. "You dream about it, remember it in weird moments, like when you're in bed with your girl, and suddenly you remember their faces, and you can't perform. Fucks with your head."

"Your daughter's name is Adelina?"

He looked surprised at the question. "Yeah."

"Adelina dos Santos?"

"You're not going to use her to blackmail me, mate? You don't need to do that."

"We don't use blackmail, Jan. That's not how we do things. Is that her name?"

"Yeah, why?"

"For the file."

He didn't look convinced. "Right..."

"What was she doing there?"

A breeze blew in off the East River, bringing a slightly rancid smell of ozone. He considered me a moment, squinting his eyes. "What has that got to do with you, or anybody?"

"Next time you dodge a question I'm going to blow your kneecap off. Do I need to prove I mean it?"

He studied my face. "No."

"What was she doing at your apartment?"

"A few years ago, when she turned eighteen, I went to see her and told her who I was. I'd pulled strings all her life to make sure she went to the best schools, university, and got a good job—"

"Who does she work for? Why is she here in New York?"

"She works for Afro-American Petrochemicals. They have an office in New York and I got them to send her here. I figured it would be good for her, professionally, and open her up to the wider, Western world."

He flicked the cigarette butt out into the water, then scratched his head.

"It hadn't gone great when I told her I was her father. She'd accused me of a lot of shit. I tried to tell her I'd always kept an eye out for her and her mother, but she didn't buy it. Women, huh? All they want is absolutely everything." I didn't laugh and he went on. "Anyway, when she arrived in New York I asked her to come and see me, so we could talk and try and sort things out."

"Why are the CIA watching you?"

He didn't look surprised. "You won't be surprised to discover that the USA's promise to elevate Cabinda-Itumba to the international stage never materialized. It has always been, and still is, a small, poor country most people have never even heard of. So I took a trip recently to Moscow at the head of a trade delegation, and arranged a private meeting at the Kremlin. There, I suggested to several top officials that we could buy things in the Western marketplace which they could not, because of the international trade embargos against Russia. However, given the right inducements, we would be willing to do so and quietly sell them on to Moscow via the back door.

"The inducements in question were along the lines of Moscow providing us with the kind of weaponry and training that would, at last, make our presence felt in Africa, if not the wider world. I don't know if you are aware of this, but President Cosmo Manuel considers that there are areas along the coast which rightfully belong to his tribe. If he had them, that could make Cabinda-Itumba an international player.

"Obviously, the CIA were not pleased about our cozying up to the Russians, and they are mad at me. They hold me responsible and think I should be taught a lesson."

I was quiet for a long time, watching the sun turn copper on the small waves. Finally I asked him: "How many villages have you annihilated, Jan?"

He shrugged. I watched him pull another cigarette from the pack and poke it in his mouth. "Six, seven. I forget." He flicked his lighter and leaned into the flame. When the cigarette was alight I said, "The tide is rising." I jerked my head at where the water line had risen and was just a couple of feet from his boots. He stared at it a moment, and somehow he understood what it meant. He frowned at me and stood, spreading his hands. "Aw, come on, you said—"

"No, you said, Jan. All I said was we take care of things while providing credible deniability, and we pay the highest rates. This is your payment for annihilating...," I echoed his shrug, "six or seven villages."

I put the slug through his right frontal lobe, so it spun him slightly, turning his back to the water. So when he fell he fell toward the rising black tide. He lay there, with his feet higher than his head, staring wide-eyed at the sky, as the pulsing water gradually covered his face. Soon, during the dark hours of the night, as the tide receded, he would be dragged out to the deep.

On an impulse I moved down to where he was lying, took my handkerchief and stuffed it in his mouth. Then, using my Swiss Army knife I cut off a chunk of his hair, folded it in the handkerchief and put it in my pocket.

I reached in his jacket, found his cell and his keys and made my way back across the scrubland to where he'd parked. There I climbed behind the wheel and drove slowly up Soundview to the Bruckner Expressway, and retraced our steps to the parking garage under 166 East 35th Street. I left the car in his lot and his key in the glove compartment, and, after a moment's thought, made my way up to his apartment and let myself in.

I had a snoop around, but there was one thing in particular I was looking for and I found it in a small bedroom he'd adapted as a den. It was his laptop. Before taking it I searched the drawers in his desk for some kind of diary. I found it. It was long, slim, black and leather-bound, as you'd expect. I opened it and smiled. All his passwords were neatly laid out in alphabetical order. The more security the nerds force on us, the sloppier they force us to become.

Downstairs I retrieved my car and sat behind the wheel for a while growing steadily more mad. Finally I pulled my cell from my pocket and dialed. The brigadier answered.

"Yes, Harry."

"Job's done. Is the colonel with you?"

"No. Why?"

"I need to talk to her about this job."

"Was there a problem?"

"Yeah, you could say there was a problem."

"We'd better meet at my flat. Four twenty-eight, Riverside Drive." He gave me the number of the apartment and asked, "How serious is this, Harry? Is there some action I need to be taking?"

"I don't know until we talk to the colonel."

"All right, come on over. If you get here before she does you can tell me what it's about."

I went home to my brownstone on James Baldwin Place, showered and shaved and changed my clothes. I guess I wasn't that keen to tell the brigadier what it was all about before the colonel showed up. Finally, at about six in the evening I took my TVR and growled across Manhattan to Morningside Heights, and rode the antique elevator up to the top floor. The brigadier opened the door himself and arched an eyebrow at me.

"I expected you a little earlier."

"Yes, sir. But I thought the least I could do was change out of my work clothes and have a shave." I noted that he was wearing a sage green, paisley silk cravat. "Has the colonel arrived?"

"Some time ago. Whiskey?"

"Thank you."

I followed him into the drawing room. The brigadier was not the kind of man to have a living room, he had a drawing room, into which one withdrew to listen to music, read books and drink very expensive drinks. I had to pause. The entire west wall was taken up with two large windows and two sliding glass doors onto an ample terrace. On the terrace now, in a violet silk dress that did nothing to hide her legs, was the colonel, holding a tall gin and tonic. She was gazing out at Riverside Park, the vast, dark Hudson and the glimmering lights of Jersey across the water.

The colonel was pouring my drink and spoke over his shoulder. "I had a feeling this might happen, so I have booked a table at Keens."

"For you and the colonel?"

He went very still, then turned to face me. He handed me my drink.

"I am going to ignore that remark, Harry. It is unworthy of you. But don't do it again."

I took the drink and nodded once. "Yes sir."

He crossed the floor to the sliding doors and leaned out.

"Jane, would you like to join us?"

She turned, stepped inside and stared at me a moment. My belly was warm with adrenalin and I told myself it was because I was mad.

She said, "Hello, Harry."

I nodded and spoke quietly. "Colonel."

She lowered herself into a large, calico chair. "The brigadier said you wanted to talk to me."

The brigadier sat on the sofa. I remained standing.

"Yeah, I'd like to know if I am being used as a hit man for the CIA."

Her face might have been granite for all the expression it showed. She met my eye and held it. "Explain yourself!"

"I don't need to explain myself, Colonel. You gave me a job, I accepted it and I did it. You and your pals at the CIA had him under surveillance. So I think you need to explain to me why you told me he was alone, but when I got there he was with a woman. Did the Company think I was going to execute her for them too? Maybe you could explain to me also why I wasn't told the Company had him on a list to be punished for cozying up to the Russians. So no, I am not going to 'explain myself,' Colonel, but I think you should explain yourself. Are you using Cobra to execute contracts for the CIA?"

She sat very still and didn't say anything. I reached in my pocket and pulled out two plastic bags, which I dropped on the lamp table beside the brigadier. One contained Adelina's small plastic bottle. The other contained the handkerchief smothered in Jan's saliva and his hair.

"The woman left, having seen my face. You had better explain to the CIA that I do not kill innocent people just because they may be able to identify me. I let her go because I had to, as a matter of moral principle. So I took Jan in his own car to Soundview Park, at the mouth of the Bronx River, and I made him talk. He told me a lot. Among other things he told me the girl was his daughter, her name is Adelina dos Santos and she works for Afro-American Petrochemicals." I pointed. "The handkerchief and the hair are his DNA. The bottle is her DNA. I want to know if she really is his daughter, I want a copy of the CIA file on him and I want to know if I have been played."

The room went quiet. The brigadier, usually quick to defuse any kind of tension, remained silent, looking down at the carpet, pursing his lips. The colonel's cheeks had turned a very attractive pink and I battled with myself to remain mad. After a moment she said, "Absolutely not."

I frowned at her. "Absolutely not, what? She is absolutely not his daughter, I absolutely cannot have a copy of the CIA file, or I absolutely cannot know if I have been played?"

She had added bright, moist eyes to her pink cheeks and was watching me with barely repressed fury. The brigadier said, "Why don't you sit down, Harry?"

He made it sound like the sanest thing to do in an insane world, so I did it. When I was safely seated and sipping my whiskey, he shifted his gaze to the colonel.

"Jane, you know you have my unconditional trust. That is how we operate. But you know also that it is not enough for justice to be done, it must be *seen* to be done. The fact is your operatives told you van Hoek was alone, when they must have known this woman was with him."

He didn't wait for her to answer. He reached for his phone, pressed a single number and after a moment said, "Send me a courier. I have some items for the lab." He hung up and made another call. "I am sending you two items. Label them A and B. A is the bottle. I want to know if the two people were related. Give it top priority. I want the results by morning."

He hung up again and looked at the colonel. There was resentment in her eyes when she returned his stare, and when she looked at me.

"I was not a part of the investigation into Jan van Hoek. I knew that the Company's interest in him centered around the rise of Russian influence in Africa, but nothing beyond that. A week ago the director had the file sent to me. He is the only person who knows about my secondment to Cobra. He called me and told me the CIA could not pursue the matter here in the States beyond simply observing the target, but that I should draw the man's record to the attention of the board at Cobra, to see if he was a suitable mark. And that is precisely what I did, Alex, with your approval, and the board unanimously agreed he should be executed."

The brigadier turned to me. "That is absolutely correct. I can vouch for every word."

I held the colonel's eye. "Why was I sent to hit van Hoek when there was a woman there with him? It could have cost me my life, and if you had sent a less experienced operative it could have cost an innocent woman *her* life. I don't believe they didn't know she was there. I don't believe the CIA are that sloppy."

"I don't know." She took a deep breath and added, "You are quite right. It should not have happened and I can assure you the CIA are *not* that sloppy. If it happened it was either a fluke or it was deliberate. Either way I'll find out and report back to you both."

I said, "Thank you. What about the copy of the file?"

She glanced at the brigadier. He frowned and cleared his throat. "What for, Harry? The job is done. There was an incident and we want to ensure it doesn't happen again. But snooping on CIA operations is not what we do, and it will set a very bad precedent."

I jerked my chin toward the two plastic bags on the lamp table beside him. "Why are you checking on van Hoek's DNA? Why do you want to know if she was his daughter?"

He gave his head a short, dismissive shake. "That is quite different, Harry. It has nothing to do with the CIA investigation. It is a legitimate part of our work to investigate the people closely related to a target, to see to what extent they are, or were, involved in the target's crimes."

I nodded and waited a moment, studying his face.

"Forgive me if I seem impertinent, sir, but I think you just answered your own question. I want to know to what extent the CIA were involved in van Hoek's crimes."

Made in the USA
Monee, IL
16 July 2025

21295097R00114